"It's the dress we made for Anna to wear when she was going to marry Olaf."

The statement ended almost in a whisper.

August turned to stare at the dress for a moment.

"I didn't know," he murmured, then glanced toward Anna. "I'm sorry I brought it up."

Anna turned to replace the folded fabric on the shelves behind the counter. "It's okay. I knew that everyone would see it when I put it in the window."

August walked over to the counter and leaned across it toward Anna. "Why are you selling the dress?"

Anna didn't turn around. She stood with one hand on the bolt of fabric so long that August thought she wasn't going to answer his question.

"I'll never wear it."

LENA NELSON DOOLEY is a free-lance author and editor who lives with her husband in Texas. During the twenty years she has been a professional writer, she has been involved as a writer or editor on a variety of projects. She developed a seminar called "Write Right," and she hosts a writing critique group in her home. She presently works full-time as an author and editor. She has a dramatic ministry and speaking ministry that crosses denominational lines and an international Christian clowning ministry. She and her husband enjoy taking vacations in Mexico, visiting and working with missionary friends.

Books by Lena Nelson Dooley

HEARTSONG PRESENTS

HP54—Home to Her Heart
HP492—The Other Brother

His Brother's Castoff

Lena Nelson Dooley

Heartsong Presents

To my two teenaged grandsons, Timothy Van Zant and Austin Waldron. You are precious to me, and I love you very much.

Special thanks go to my wonderful husband, James. Without your support, no book would be written in our home. Thank you for loving me and allowing me to be all that God intends.

A note from the Author:
I love to hear from my readers! You may correspond with me by writing:

Lena Nelson Dooley
Author Relations
PO Box 719
Uhrichsville, OH 44683

ISBN 1-59310-078-7

HIS BROTHER'S CASTOFF

Our mission is to publish and distribute inspirational products offering exceptional value and biblical encouragement to the masses.

All Scripture quotations are taken from the King James Version of the Bible.

PRINTED IN THE U.S.A.

one

Minnesota—September 1894

Fingers of early morning sunlight slipped between the panels of heavy draperies and bathed Anna Jenson's face with warmth. She slowly opened her eyes, then squeezed them tight against the brightness. Sitting up against her pillows, she stretched her arms above her head and smiled. She pulled her heavy dark braid across her shoulder and began at the bottom to carefully work the hair loose from its confinement. Then she ran her fingers through the soft length to be sure there were no tangles.

Today was a special day. Gerda Nilsson and Merta Petersson were coming to help Anna work on her wedding dress. Gerda and her sister-in-law Olina had helped design the gorgeous gown. They also ordered the fabric from Paris. For the first time in her life, Anna would wear silk. She felt beautiful just thinking about walking down the aisle with the material swishing around her.

Finally, she would be married. One month from today. She pictured her fiancé, Olaf Johanson, with the unruly black curls that danced across his forehead. Kind, steady Olaf, whose blue eyes twinkled when he smiled at her. They would have a good life together. His farm wasn't as large as her father's, but it would be able to support them and the family they would have.

Anna wondered how many children God would bless

them with. Maybe she would have a baby by this time next year. She hoped it wouldn't take too long. She wanted a boy first. A boy with his father's dark curls and twinkling eyes. Maybe a girl would be next. Of course, it didn't matter which came first, but she hoped she would have both sons and daughters. Olaf would have to build on to the tiny farmhouse to make room for their children. She looked forward to their planning together the addition to their home.

Shaking her head, Anna got up and started dressing. She couldn't stay in bed daydreaming about her wonderful life with Olaf. If she did, she wouldn't be ready when her dress arrived. Gerda and Olina had made it using their sewing machine. This would be the first time Anna would try it on since they stitched it together. Today she would get to see what she looked like in the beautiful gown.

Of course there was still a lot of handwork to be done on the dress. That was why Gerda and Merta were coming. The three friends would sew yards and yards of lace on the skirt. Anna looked forward to finishing the special garment, but she also anticipated spending time with her two best friends. The three young women always had a lot of things to talk about. Since both Gerda and Merta lived in Litchfield, they could catch her up on all the new happenings in town.

Anna hurried down the stairs, almost skipping because she was so happy. When she entered the kitchen, she was surprised. No one was there except her mother.

"Where is everyone?"

Margreta Jenson looked up from the piecrust she was rolling out. A smudge of flour decorated one of her cheeks. "They've all eaten and gone out to see about the horses."

"So early?" Anna picked up a slice of apple her mother had prepared to put in the crust and sucked the cinnamon and sugar from it before popping it into her mouth.

"It's not so early, for sure. You slept a little late today, Anna." Margreta smiled at her only daughter. "There is some food for you in the warming oven."

Anna hugged her mother. "*Tack så mycket,* I mean, thank you very much. Sometimes I forget to speak English, even after all these years."

"I do, too." Her mother nodded. "But Soren wants us to use English. It helps us when we are around other people. America is our home now, not Sweden."

"Father is right." Anna folded up a large dish towel and used it to protect her hand from the heat while she lifted the warm plate from the oven. "It smells good, and I'm hungry."

"When do you think Gerda and Merta will arrive?"

Anna poured herself a glass of milk and brought it to the table. "I'm not sure. Probably as soon as they are finished with cleaning up after breakfast, so I need to eat quickly." After bowing her head for a brief prayer, she took a bite of the still-warm biscuit that dripped with melted butter. She couldn't keep from licking a wayward drop from her thumb, even though her mother would say it wasn't polite if she had seen her do it. Thankfully, Mother was fitting the crust into the pie tin.

The sound of a carriage coming down the drive interrupted Anna before she took her last drink of milk. "It sounds as though they are here." She gathered her dishes and took them over to the sink.

Before she started running water in the dishpan, her mother said, "Don't bother with that, Anna." Margreta placed the apple pie into the oven. "I'll wash your dishes while I'm cleaning up from this pie."

Anna glanced at her. "Are you sure?"

"*Ja,* for sure. You go be with your friends." Margreta used both hands to shoo her daughter from the kitchen.

Anna was thankful to have such a wonderful mother. She hoped that when she had children she would do as good a job.

❧

"So, what do you think?" Gerda looked up and down Anna's body, checking how the dress fit.

Anna turned slowly and looked over her shoulder. She could only see part of the dress in the mirror at one time, so she moved around to get the whole picture. She liked what she saw. The full skirt rippled with every move she made. Because she was taller and had a larger frame than most of the girls she knew, she always felt awkward and less feminine. This dress did something to her figure that made it look graceful.

She smiled at Gerda. "It's more beautiful than I imagined it would be." Anna grabbed her friend and gave her a big hug.

Gerda pulled back. "I don't want to crush it. Now take it off, and we'll start sewing on the lace."

Anna went behind the screen her mother had moved into the parlor for her to use while they worked on the dress. As she changed into her regular clothes, she thought about the reflection of herself in the wedding gown. Everyone would be surprised when she walked down the aisle. She could imagine Olaf's stunned expression when he first saw her coming toward him. A special spark—of passion perhaps—would light his beautiful eyes. It would be wonderful—a moment Anna would cherish all her life.

"Anna," Gerda called to her. "I brought several pieces of lace for you to choose from. I thought we might put some around the neckline and even on the sleeves."

Anna stepped around the screen. "Let me see what you have."

Gerda was sitting on the settee with several pieces of the lace in her lap. Some were round medallions, some diamond shaped or irregular. Merta had lifted one and held it up to the light from the window. It was curved at the top and fell into a V-shape.

"This would be beautiful on the bodice, at the neckline."

The three friends chose what lace to use and pinned it to the dress. Then they started sewing it on, using tiny, almost invisible stitches. Gerda worked on the bodice while Merta and Anna added lacy ruffles to the skirt.

Gerda glanced up from her work. "Anna, it's so good to see you happy."

Anna looked up and smiled. "I am happy, and it's wonderful."

Gerda hesitated, as if she were afraid to go on. Anna could tell that something was on her friend's mind.

"What did you want to say to me? We've been friends long enough to be honest with each other, haven't we?"

Gerda nodded and bent over her sewing. "I'm glad you were able to get over the hurt my brother caused."

"That's ancient history, Gerda." Anna knew that deep inside there was a painful place that wouldn't go away, but she didn't want to think about it right now. "Gustaf and Olina are so right for each other. I know that."

Merta tied off her thread. She snipped it close to the fabric, then started threading her needle again. "You know, I was surprised when you and Gustaf started keeping time together."

Anna looked at her with a questioning expression. "Why do you say that?"

"You remember that my family came to America right before the Nilssons did. When they first arrived, I thought August was the one who was interested in you."

"August?" Anna and Gerda said in unison. Both of the young women laughed.

"Yes." Merta sounded positive.

Gerda shook her head. "August has always been so shy. Why would you think he was interested in Anna?"

"He was always looking at her, especially if he thought no one would notice. His eyes had a longing expression in them." Merta started sewing again. "I saw it several times. I kept waiting for him to say something to you."

Gerda laughed. "August wasn't like that. I think you're imagining things."

"Maybe so." Merta sounded doubtful.

And maybe not. Anna remembered many times when she had caught August looking at her. Even on the night when Gustaf had broken off their relationship. There was a party at the community center. Many times that night Anna had felt as though someone was staring at her, and when she looked up, it was August. She had passed it off at the time, but could he have been interested in her? If he was, why hadn't he said something after Gustaf stopped coming over? That would have been a good time to start a relationship, but he had done nothing to indicate that he was interested in her. Well, it was too late now. One month from today, she would become Mrs. Olaf Johanson.

The young women worked together most of the day so they could finish the dress. At noon, Mrs. Jenson brought tea and delicate sandwiches into the parlor. She ate with them and caught up with what was going on in town. Anna was glad that her mother had a good relationship with her friends. The four of them enjoyed visiting and sharing. This had been true as long as Anna could remember.

When everyone was through eating the sandwiches, Margreta brought pound cake for dessert. After lunch, she went to town to do some shopping.

Around midafternoon, the last stitch was made in the

beautiful gown. Anna tried it on again. With the addition of the various pieces of lace, Anna was awestruck by her reflection in the mirror. The time before her wedding couldn't go by fast enough for her.

After thanking her friends once again for their diligent work, she stood on the porch and watched them drive down toward the road. She carefully took her wedding gown upstairs to her bedroom and hung it in the wardrobe.

Anna returned to the parlor. She had just finished putting her needles, thread, and scissors into the sewing basket when she heard someone ride up on a horse. Someone who was in a big hurry. Anna felt sorry for the horse's having to run so fast, even if summer's heat had given way to the milder weather in September. After going to the window, she peeked out through the lace curtains.

Olaf was stepping onto the porch. Anna went into the foyer and opened the front door.

"Come in." Anna smiled up at him. Although she was tall, he towered above her. His twinkling eyes smiled down at hers.

Olaf carelessly put one arm across her shoulders and dropped a casual kiss on her cheek. Anna wished he would kiss her more romantically. It was only a month until they would be married. Surely a different kiss would be in order. But Olaf was a perfect gentleman when he was with her. Maybe too much of a gentleman. Anna wanted him to exhibit some passion about her and their approaching marriage. It had taken him a year to ask her to marry him, and then he wanted to wait over nine months for the wedding. Somehow his affection for her felt lukewarm, not passionate. She wondered what it would be like to have Olaf sweep her into his arms and kiss her the way she had seen her father kiss her mother when they didn't know anyone was watching.

Anna put her arm around Olaf's waist as they walked to the parlor. "You seem to be in a hurry."

"I wanted to tell you my good news." It was evident that Olaf was excited about something. Maybe something about the wedd— Before she finished that thought, he continued. "Angus McPherson has asked me to guide him on a hunting trip into Montana."

"Who is Angus McPherson?" Anna stepped back and folded her arms. Why in the world did that make him so excited? For some reason, she had an uncomfortable feeling in the pit of her stomach, almost as if something were wrong. *Lord, please, not now.* The thought came before she could stop it. The dread started to build until it almost consumed her. She could taste it. She tried to push it down, but it continued to grow.

"He's a man who has come over from Scotland because he heard about the good elk hunting in Montana." Olaf reached to push back a tangle of black curls that had fallen across his brow, almost covering his eyes.

All Anna could think about was that Olaf needed a haircut soon. She hoped he would get one before the wedding. "Just when will this hunting trip take place?" She was thinking of everything that still needed to be done before the wedding. Since she was the only daughter in the family, her mother wanted it to be special. And Anna did, too. She thought Olaf agreed with her, but now she wasn't so sure.

He placed both his hands in the back pockets of his waist overalls and rocked on the balls of his feet before he answered. "We leave on Monday." He looked at the floor instead of at her. It felt as if he didn't want to see her reaction. He must have known she wouldn't be happy about it.

"And how long will you be gone on this trip?" Why was it so hard to get all the details from Olaf? They never communicated the way she and Gustaf had. Why was she thinking about Gustaf at a time like this? She had been over him for a long time. She was glad he and Olina were so happy. Their daughter was a year old, and Olina was expecting their second child. Anna helped with little Olga whenever she could.

"It will take at least three weeks." Olaf rubbed the carpet with the toe of his boot, outlining the floral design. Was he trying to wear a hole in the rug?

"Three weeks!" Anna knew that she sounded like a shrew, but she couldn't help raising her voice. She placed her fisted hands on her hips the same way her mother did when she was upset. "Our wedding is only a month away."

"Aw, Anna." Olaf took hold of her shoulders with both hands. Finally, he looked at her. "I know when the wedding is, and I'm looking forward to it as much as you are." He gathered her into his arms and leaned his chin on the top of her head. He held her a moment before he continued. "But this is a chance for me to make a lot of money. It'll really help us. I can start adding on to the house soon after the wedding."

Anna leaned back in his arms and looked up at his face, once again wishing he would pull her into a passionate kiss. "Olaf, please don't go. I have a bad feeling about it. Please stay here. . .because you love me."

Olaf flung himself away from Anna and went out into the foyer, the force of his boot heels making loud drumbeats on the wooden floor. Then he turned to look back at her. "You know that I love you, Anna." His voice boomed through the nearly empty house, and the words didn't sound loving. He had never spoken so harshly to her before. "But I am going on this trip."

"Do you, Olaf?" Anna shouted, trying not to cry. "Do you really love me?"

Olaf jerked the door open, banging it so hard against the wall that Anna was afraid the glass would break. Before he exited, he told her in a monotone voice, "I'm not going to be controlled by a woman, not even one I love. I'm not going to live my life that way, so we should start our life together the right way. I love you, Anna, and I promise I'll be back in plenty of time for the wedding."

He slammed the door behind him and stomped across the porch. He didn't even kiss her good-bye. Anna felt sorry for the horse as Olaf jumped into the saddle and galloped away. She leaned back against the door and covered her mouth with her hand to stifle a sob. One thing gave her a little hope. Olaf had promised to be back for the wedding, and Olaf never broke his promises.

two

October

August Nilsson bent over the anvil in his blacksmith shop in Litchfield, pounding a horseshoe. Although a cool breeze blew through the large open doorway, the fire in the massive forge and his own hard work caused sweat to run down his forehead. He swiped at it with the back of his hand. Then he reached into the hip pocket of his denim overalls and pulled out a bandanna. He wiped the sweat from his forehead and the back of his neck before hanging the bandanna from his back pocket.

August liked working with molten iron. His arms had grown powerful as he beat it into shape time after time. No one knew that his aggressive strokes were fueled by more than just the need to create useful things. No one knew that he fought against jealousy every day of his life. Jealousy that burned as hot as the flames in the forge. Jealousy that threatened to destroy him if he didn't keep it under control.

For years he had carried on this battle within—losing more often than he cared to admit, even to himself. Everyone thought of August as the quiet Nilsson brother. He never gave anyone any trouble. He was a model of decorum, at least outwardly.

His younger brother, Lars, had always gotten into one scrape after another. August often wondered if Lars would ever grow up. It had taken him years to settle down. He finally did, but he had left a path strewn with colossal messes, not the least of which was the one when he had sent

Olina Sandstrom the money to come to America to marry him. Before she arrived, he had already moved to Denver and married another woman. August had been surprised when Olina forgave Lars. Everything had finally worked out when Olina and Gustaf married.

Gustaf was the older brother. The perfect older brother. The brother August had been jealous of most of his life.

He wasn't sure when it had started. Maybe something happened when he was very young, something he couldn't even remember. But he knew that the jealousy always had been there, eating away at him. As he grew older, he tried to control it, but he was never able to completely destroy it. The jealousy was like a disease with no cure.

The Nilsson family had immigrated to America. August was still in his teens when they came to Minnesota from Sweden. He was the only one in the family who hadn't wanted to leave their native country, but he didn't express his opinion in the family discussions before they came. After all, he was the quiet one. No one expected him to have any objections. Everyone else was so set on coming. Especially Gustaf. And Gustaf usually got what he wanted. *Ja*, that was for sure.

The first time the Nilsson family attended church in America, August lost his heart to Anna Jenson. He tried not to let anyone know that he was watching her, but he was aware of every move she made. She was tall, with dark hair cascading down her back that first time he saw her. Before long, she had started wearing it up, as the other young women did, but August had never forgotten how it looked, swinging as she walked, barely brushing her hips.

August was not as tall as Gustaf, but even at nineteen, he was a big man. That's why he made such a good blacksmith. He was strong and muscular. But he was also shy. So he quietly studied Anna every time he was near her, trying to work up the courage to talk to her. He liked the fact that she was tall and strong.

August had never been interested in small girls. He felt clumsy around them. He was afraid he would hurt them without meaning to. Even though she wasn't dainty, Anna had a grace about her—not like some tall women who slumped to appear shorter. He liked everything about her.

Before he worked up the courage to speak to Anna for the first time, Gustaf sat beside her and introduced himself. She had smiled up at him. August liked watching her eyes flash, and a smile spread across her face as she talked. Why couldn't he be like Gustaf? He should have spoken to her first. Then she would have been smiling up at him instead of his brother.

After that first day when Gustaf spoke to her, Anna had not paid attention to any other man. She had followed him around every time they went to church. Soon she and Gerda had become best friends. They spent a lot of time together, either at the Nilsson farm or at the Jensons'. August tried to harden his heart against her, but when no one was looking, he feasted his eyes on her beauty, wishing he were his older brother so she would notice him.

After a couple of years, Gustaf and Anna started keeping time together. Since then August had a major, ongoing battle with the jealousy. He would pray, begging God to take it away. But the next time he saw Anna and Gustaf together, there it would be, making its way back into his heart. He was glad when his father let him move to town and apprentice as a blacksmith. He didn't see Gustaf as often, so he was able to control the jealousy a little more.

"Are you trying to beat that horseshoe to death?" Gustaf's voice penetrated August's dark thoughts.

August stopped what he was doing, took the bandanna from his back pocket, and wiped the sweat from his face again before he turned toward the doorway. "That iron doesn't shape itself, you know." Gustaf laughed with August. "What brings you to the smithy? Do you have something I need to fix?"

Gustaf dusted off the front of the work table that was next to the wall, then leaned against it. "Can't I just come to visit my brother?"

"*Ja,* for sure." August stuffed the bandanna back into his pocket. As he joined Gustaf against the table, he crossed his arms over his chest, placing his hands under the opposite arms. "So how's Olina doing?" Whenever he was with Gustaf, he was better able to control his emotions. It was after Gustaf left that the tormenting thoughts would do battle in his mind.

Gustaf shook his head. "This time she has a lot more morning sickness. It's hard on her, since she has to take care of Olga, too."

"But she's okay, isn't she?" August really cared about his sister-in-law.

"*Ja, Mor* assures me this is normal." August was sure that Gustaf was glad their mother lived so close so she could help sometimes. "I wish I could take some of it away from her. I want to protect her."

August wondered what it would feel like to have a woman to love and cherish. Would he ever know that feeling? He couldn't imagine ever loving a woman the way Gustaf loved Olina.

The two men shared a moment of companionable silence before August asked another question. "So, how's my favorite niece?"

"You mean your only niece, don't you?" Gustaf chuckled. "Now that Olga is walking all over the place, Olina has her hands full. That's why I don't come to town as much as I used to. When I'm not at the farm helping Fader, I stay home to give Olina some relief. And Olga loves me. When I come home, she runs across the room with her arms outstretched and wants me to pick her up, even before I have time to clean up."

A stab of jealousy penetrated August's carefully constructed defenses. Here he was twenty-six years old, and still he had no family. If Gustaf hadn't spent so much time with Anna, maybe he would have spoken to her. Maybe he would be the one with a wife and child—and another on the way.

When Gustaf broke off his relationship with Anna, August could have tried to establish one with her. But jealousy raised its ugly head. He didn't want his brother's castoff. If he hadn't fought jealousy so long, maybe he would have started something with Anna that could have led to a permanent relationship. Before he was able to overcome his aversion to having Gustaf's leftovers, Olaf Johanson had already captured Anna's affections.

"Well, I only stopped by to tell you that Gerda is staying at the house to fix supper tonight so that Olina won't have to. She told me to ask you to come." Gustaf stood away from the table and brushed off the back of his trousers.

"I won't turn down a home-cooked meal; that's for sure." August got tired of eating at the boardinghouse, and he wasn't able to cook in his room. Occasionally, he would go to the hotel dining room to eat, but by far his favorite place to eat was at the house of one of his relatives. And Gerda was a wonderful cook. This would be a good evening, getting to see Olga and having a home-cooked meal.

As Gustaf ambled out the door, August picked up the horseshoe with the tongs and held it in the flames of the forge. While he watched the iron change color, he fought the demons that threatened to consume him, bringing them under control once again. Sometimes it was very hard to do, and today was one of those days. He didn't want them to accompany him to his brother's house later and ruin the evening for him.

❧

When August started to knock on the door of Gustaf and Olina's house, he heard Olga shriek with glee. Probably Gustaf was teasing her or chasing her. She liked to be chased. Her little legs would pump as she rushed across the room, often falling into a heap of laughter. Someday maybe he would have a daughter.

Before his knuckles connected with the door, it flew open. Gerda looked into his face, laughing. "Come in, August. You're just in time for all the fun."

August stepped inside. Olga looked up at him and laughed out loud. She put her hands on the floor and pushed her little bottom into the air before she stood up. Then she rushed toward him with her arms outstretched.

"Unka, Unka, up!"

August bent down and grasped her under her arms. He lifted her into a high arc that ended with him showering her neck with kisses as he gathered her close to his chest. By the time he was through, they were both breathless with laughter.

"Is anyone hungry?" Gerda looked from one brother to the other. "Or are you going to spend all evening playing?"

"August, it's good to see you." Olina descended the stairs, looking regal, but a little pale. She stood on tiptoe and kissed his cheek, then took her daughter from his arms. "Come, Olga. Let's eat supper."

After they finished eating, August told Gustaf and Olina that he would help Gerda clean up. He enjoyed spending time with his sister. She kept him up on what was going on better than anyone else did.

After she had told him all about what was happening on the farm, he asked, "So how is the dressmaking business?"

"We're very busy." Gerda hung the tea towel on the edge of the cabinet and took off her apron. "It's hard to keep up with all the orders." She leaned close to him and whispered, "I'm trying to protect Olina from having to do much. She gets tired so easily."

August nodded. "I can see that. Have you thought about getting someone else to help out?"

August pulled out a chair from the table and sat in it. Gerda did the same.

"I thought about asking Anna, but she is working so hard on the wedding. And then she will have a home of her own to take care of."

❧

Olaf Johanson kept his promise to Anna. He returned before the wedding. Two days before the wedding. But he wasn't riding his horse. He came home in the bed of a wagon, completely wrapped in canvas. Even his face.

Now Anna knew why she'd had such a bad feeling about the hunting trip. Maybe God was trying to tell her something. She had never been able to get that thought to dissipate the whole time Olaf was gone. Why couldn't he have listened to her when she tried to tell him? Had he ever cared about her feelings? Perhaps their whole marriage would have been that way, with him trying to control her and not letting her express who she was and what she felt.

Here she was on what was supposed to be her wedding day, getting ready to go to her fiancé's funeral. Her white silk dress was carefully packed away in a trunk, and she wore black wool gabardine. She wasn't even eligible to wear widow's weeds, because she wasn't a widow. But she felt like one. Once again, her heart had been ripped to shreds.

The service was held in the community center out on the prairie. Olaf's parents didn't want the funeral to be in the white clapboard church in town. They had only gone there on rare occasions, instead preferring the family feel of the services held in the structure that was so near their farm. Anna hadn't even had any say in the plans for the service. She would have preferred that the funeral be held in the building in town. It seemed more like a church than this one did. She couldn't keep from remembering all the parties she had attended here.

The edifice was used as a schoolhouse and for community functions as well as for church. The last time Anna had been here was for a party. The room had been draped with gaily colored paper streamers. Today it was so stark. Stark and cold. Cold and dreary.

At the front of the room, Olaf's handcrafted pine box was covered with autumn leaves, since it was too late for any flowers. Actually, there weren't many leaves left either. It had taken Anna and Gerda a long time to find enough to cover the top of the casket. At least his family had let her take care of that detail.

During the service, Anna sat on the front bench beside Mrs. Johanson. Gerda sat beside her. Anna didn't think she would have been able to get through this without Gerda's friendship. Tears trailed down Anna's cheeks, and Gerda pressed a handkerchief into Anna's hand. She wiped her tears away and returned the handkerchief before they filed out of the building, following the pallbearers to the open wound in the ground.

When they stood beside the grave and listened to the preacher recite the Lord's Prayer, Anna couldn't remember what had gone on during the service inside the building. It was a blur in her mind. Everything since Olaf's body arrived home was a blur. Everything except the pain in her heart. That pain was focused and sharp and penetrating.

Why were her last words to Olaf spoken in anger? Why hadn't he loved her enough to listen to her warning? She didn't even want to think about what this day should have been.

When the graveside service was over, Gerda guided Anna back inside the building. Several women had turned the community center into a place to serve dinner to the family and friends of Olaf. Although the room was still stark and bare, the smell of food permeated every corner. Anna looked at the table spread with a bounty of dishes, and her stomach churned. She fought back the feeling of nausea. Hadn't enough happened without her throwing up in front of everyone?

"May I fill a plate for you?" Gerda sat in the chair beside Anna.

Anna shook her head. "Not now. I couldn't eat a thing."

Gerda patted her hand. "If there is anything I can do, just tell me."

Anna nodded without speaking, tears streaming down her cheeks again. Gerda took another pristine white handkerchief from her pocket and handed it to Anna. She must have known that Anna would need more than one.

❧

When the men finished shoveling the dirt on the coffin in the grave, they came into the building for something to eat. They had worked up a good appetite both digging the grave that morning and then covering it up after the service.

August looked around the room and saw his sister with Anna. He was glad Gerda was there for her. Anna needed someone right now. His gaze traveled from her hands twisting a soggy handkerchief to her face that was still wet from tears. In his opinion, even the red blotches could not take away from her beauty. His heart constricted at her pain. He wished he could shoulder it for her and shelter her from this storm that life had raged against her.

Lustrous, abundant dark brown hair framed her face. The black hat could not hide the highlights that gleamed in the sunlight streaming through the window. August was sure her hair must feel silky and smooth. It had been so long since he had seen Anna with her hair down, but sometimes a stray curl would make its way from her carefully constructed hairstyle. He would love to see her hair hanging in waves again. He wished it was his right. For a moment August was lost in a fantasy world, and the jealousy receded, but it didn't depart.

When he came to his senses, he realized that his thoughts were probably inappropriate. How could he fantasize about Anna when it was the day of her fiancé's funeral? What kind of man did that? August didn't really want to know, and he didn't want to be that man. He gave himself a mental shake.

"Are you going to eat anything?" Gustaf sat beside August and interrupted his thoughts.

"I was waiting until everyone else had filled their plates." August didn't take his eyes off of Anna.

"So you can eat all that's left?" The often shared joke didn't lighten August's mood, but he agreed out of habit.

Before taking a bite, Gustaf followed August's gaze across the room. "What's so interesting about our sister?"

"What?" August looked at Gustaf. *What was he talking about?*

"Or maybe it isn't our sister who has captured your interest." Gustaf turned back toward his plate and lifted a fork full of mashed sweet potatoes.

August got up and went to the table. Anna's two brothers, Lowell and Ollie, were filling their plates.

"Do you think Anna is going to be all right?" August tried to sound casual.

Lowell, the brother who was a year older than Anna, stopped putting food on his plate and stared at August. "What do you mean?"

That surprised August. He took a minute to think about his answer. "I just wondered. Today was supposed to be her wedding day, wasn't it?"

Ollie, a year younger than Anna, nodded. "So what?"

"Well. . ." August was having a hard time putting his thoughts into words. "It might be extra hard on her, losing Olaf that way. . ." He stood there with an empty plate, trying to think of something else to say.

Lowell and Ollie both turned back to piling food on their plates. They didn't seem to be bothered by what was going on with Anna, and they must have dismissed August's question. Suddenly, August's appetite left him. He stared down at his empty plate, then at the long table of food. He could have his choice of almost any food he liked, but after putting only a few spoonfuls on the plate, he returned to his seat by Gustaf.

"What's the matter, Brother? Have you lost your appetite?" Gustaf glanced at August's nearly empty dish.

"I guess I worked too hard today. Nothing looked that good." But that wasn't quite true. Something looked good to August, but it didn't have anything to do with food.

three

November

Two weeks. It had been two weeks since the funeral. Where had the time gone? Anna pulled back the curtains and opened the window. A cool autumn breeze brought fresh air into the oppressive bedroom. She had spent most of the time mourning in this space. This place that had often been a refuge for her now felt more like a prison cell. She had cried a lake full of tears, and now she felt empty. Empty and used up. Would the pain ever come to an end?

Anna wanted a change, but what? Could anything alter what happened to her? She opened the door of her wardrobe and looked at all the finery there. It bulged with more clothing than most women she knew owned. But Anna loved to sew. She often designed new frocks for herself or her mother. It had been a long time since she had felt like dressing up. She had worn the same old dark, dreary black or brown dresses too long.

Somehow today she couldn't put either of them back on. They lay in a heap on the floor in the corner of her bedroom, a quiet testimony to her tragedy. It didn't seem right to wear anything bright or fashionable, but she had to wear something. Maybe an older house dress.

As her hand hovered over the garments in the polished oak wardrobe, her gaze was drawn to her riding clothes. Although the family made their living raising horses, she hadn't been on her mare in a long time. Anna knew that the open air would do her good. Maybe it would freshen her outlook a little. . .if anything could.

Ollie was mucking out the stalls when Anna walked through the open door of the barn. He leaned the crook of his arm on the handle of the pitchfork and pulled a bandanna from the back pocket of his denim trousers to wipe the sweat from his forehead. "Hi, Sis, what're you doing here?"

"What does it look like I'm doing?" As soon as the words slipped between her lips, Anna was sorry that her voice sounded so sharp. She was able to soften it when she continued. "I'm going for a ride."

Ollie smiled as he pushed the hanky back into his pocket and leaned the pitchfork against the stall door. "Do you want me to saddle your horse for you?"

"I have been saddling my own horse since I was nine years old. I haven't forgotten how." This time she was able to force a more teasing tone into her words.

Ollie picked up the pitchfork and thrust the tines under a mound of soiled straw. "Okay. I was just trying to help."

Anna led her mare out of the stall and placed the saddle blanket on her back. When she lifted the saddle to the back of the horse, the creak of the leather was comforting. Comforting and familiar.

"I know you were. Thanks for caring." She gave Ollie the best smile she could muster. She hoped it was enough to keep him from worrying about her.

After leading Buttermilk out into the sunshine, she mounted and turned the horse away from the house. At first, Anna rode at a slow pace, but soon she and the mare flew across the prairie. This had been one of her favorite pastimes since she was old enough to ride alone. She always thought it was the closest to flying a person could ever get. The wind tugged tendrils of hair from the scarf where she had tied it at the nape of her neck. She turned her face in the wind, trying to keep the hair from blowing in her eyes.

Almost before she realized it, Buttermilk turned toward a copse of trees by a gentle stream. They had ridden this way many times before. Had she subconsciously given the horse signals that brought them to this place, or had Buttermilk come here out of habit?

Now, nearly empty branches swayed in the gentle breeze, and leaves covered the ground. Anna and Olaf had often met here. They had seen all the seasons of the year pass by. Anna loved spring with the new green leaves brushing the sky with promise. In summer, the trees had given welcome shade from the hot sun. Even when snow covered the ground and ice outlined the branches, Anna loved this place. But autumn was her least favorite season. In her mind, it symbolized death—the ending of the wonderful life of summer. How appropriate that it was autumn, for death had come into her life, in more ways than one.

In spring and summer, Anna and Olaf usually sat on a large rock beside the stream. In the winter, it had been too dangerous and cold. It was while sitting on that rock watching a beautiful sunset that Olaf asked her to marry him. Why had she come here today? It opened the wounds she was trying to ignore.

Buttermilk slowed her pace as she neared the grove, leaves crunching under her hooves. When they were close to the rock, the horse stopped and bent her head to munch the blades of brown grass that peeked through the carpet of autumn leaves. Anna slid from the horse's back and walked to the rock, but she didn't sit on it. As she stared at the monolith, anger simmered within her. She picked up a dead twig and fiddled with it, breaking small pieces off and dropping them as she stomped up the trail worn around the side of the huge stone. When she reached the flat surface at the top, she stood and looked all around. In every direction, things looked as if they were dying or were already dead.

"Olaf, why did you leave me?" Anna spit the words out as if she couldn't get rid of them quickly enough.

She picked up a small stone that had broken off from the larger block and threw it into the clear water that gurgled below. The splash sent up a spray that fell back into the stream like raindrops. Cleansing raindrops. If only something could cleanse the pain from her heart.

"Why were you so stubborn?" This time, the words were louder, and tears began to make tracks down her cheeks. But they were tears of anger, not tears of grief.

Slowly she picked her way down the side of the rock. With each step, the word *Why?* beat a cadence in her brain. She wanted to hit something. . .or someone. Actually, she wanted to hit Olaf for leaving her. She wanted him to hold her in his arms as she beat furiously against his muscular chest. But he wasn't here. He would never be here again. She leaned over and picked up a rock that peeked out from under the leaves.

"Why couldn't you love me more?" she shouted, as she threw the rock against the large stone.

Again and again, shouted questions accompanied the missiles she hurled against the monument to her unfulfilled love. Each one shattered, just as her heart had shattered. Finally, when her anger was spent, Anna stopped the barrage of words and weapons. She slumped against a tree, exhausted.

Twice she had given her heart freely, and twice it had been broken. No more. She would never give her heart to a man again. She would never risk being this hurt again. She didn't need a man. She could take care of herself.

Anna walked downstream until she came to a spot where

there was a narrow sandbar and she could walk to the water's edge. She pulled the scarf from her hair and dipped a corner of the cotton square into the cold water. With the dampened fabric, she washed the dried tears from her face. After wringing the cloth out, she tied her hair back again. Straightening her shoulders, she went to Buttermilk and caressed the beloved animal's neck before mounting and riding toward home. She sat tall in the saddle and held her head high. Today, Anna was determined that her world would change. But deep inside, somehow she knew that this would be hard to accomplish.

❧

Gerda was sitting at the kitchen table talking to Mrs. Jenson when Anna came in from the barn. "Anna, there you are. I was about to give up on you and go home."

Anna looked at her mother. "I'm sorry I didn't tell you what I was doing. I decided to go for a ride this morning." She looked at her best friend. "And I would have waited if I had known you were coming today."

"That's wonderful." Gerda jumped up and hugged her. "It's the first time you've been out of the house, isn't it?"

Anna nodded. "I know. I was becoming a recluse. I'm through with that. Today is a new day." She hoped that Gerda wouldn't recognize the emptiness in her eyes or the forced bravado in her voice.

Taking Gerda's arm, Anna escorted her into the parlor. The last time they sat in this room was when they worked on her wedding dress, but she wouldn't let herself think about that today. Hopefully, she would be able to forget that whole time in her life. She needed to move on. . .if she could.

"I should have asked while we were still in the kitchen," Anna said before she sat on the sofa. "Would you like a cup of tea? I think there are some muffins left from breakfast.

That's unusual, since Lowell and Ollie eat so much to keep up their strength."

"They're big men." Gerda smiled. "Big men eat a lot to keep them going. Right?" She looked back toward the kitchen. "I love your *moder*'s muffins. Maybe I'll eat one."

Anna smiled, and the two young women headed back to get the food. When they returned to the parlor, Anna set the tray on the table in front of the sofa. After sitting beside Gerda, she poured two cups of the fragrant brew and handed one to her friend. Then she put fresh butter on the still warm muffin and set the small plate beside Gerda's saucer.

"So what brings you by this morning?" Anna stopped suddenly. "That's a silly question. You've been faithful about checking on me every couple of days."

Gerda sipped her tea, then set the cup on the saucer. "Was I that obvious?"

"Actually, I appreciate the love you've shown me. And the understanding. I needed both of them." Anna patted Gerda's hand. "But I turned a corner this morning, I think. I'm going to be all right."

Gerda stood and walked to the window and fiddled with the lace curtains. After turning around, she straightened the crocheted doily under the lamp on the table that was framed by the curtains. Was she nervous? Anna wondered what she had to be nervous about.

"Actually, Anna, I wanted to talk to you about something. I wasn't sure I should, but since you seem better this morning—"

"I would do anything for you, just as you would for me."

Gerda came back around the end of the sofa and dropped down to sit on the edge, turning to face Anna. "The only thing that's wrong with me is that I need you to help with the dressmaking business."

"What about Olina?" Anna knew that Gerda's sister-in-law was also her partner. Besides that, the business was located in the front room of the home Olina and Gustaf Nilsson lived in on the outskirts of Litchfield.

"You know she's going to have a baby. She gets tired quicker with this one, and she has her daughter to take care of. Little Olga can be a big handful sometimes. That's for sure." Gerda laughed. "So if you could help me, it would relieve Olina a lot."

Anna sat a moment lost in thought. Did she want to work? Why not? She was good at making clothing, and it would help her move on with her life. A change of scenery might take her mind off her problems.

"When do you want me to start. . .if I decide to help?"

Gerda smiled and relaxed against the back of the sofa. Had she been afraid to ask Anna? Maybe that was why she seemed nervous earlier.

"Any time you're ready," Gerda said. "Tomorrow wouldn't be too soon."

"All right. I'll be there in the morning if you're sure Olina won't mind."

Gerda hugged Anna. "I talked it over with her before I came. She'll be glad to have the help, too."

"And we work so well together. Remember all the parties we've planned, and we've helped each other make clothing before." *A wedding dress among them.* But Anna shut that thought out of her mind. It was 1894, and in this modern time, more women were working outside the home. Tomorrow she would enter the world of business.

❧

August hurried to finish shoeing the horse Gustaf had left with him. Then he was going to clean up and ride the horse to Gustaf's house. Gerda had asked him to come by the Nilsson home for lunch today. She was fixing the meal so Olina wouldn't have to, and she wanted August to eat with them.

He walked the horse to the livery and tied it in a stall before he went to his room. For some reason, he felt like sprucing up a bit. After a good washup in his room, he got some hot water for a shave. It was unlike him to shave in the middle of the day, but he hadn't shaved that morning, and he didn't want to look like a mountain man or trapper when he went to eat. Gerda was always teasing him about his bad habit of not being careful about his grooming.

While August swished his brush around the bar of soap in his shaving mug, he whistled a happy tune. He smeared the foamy suds over his face. Then he opened his straight razor and started by sliding it up his neck. He was glad that he had stropped his razor at the end of his last shave. Its sharp edge sliced through the softened hairs as if they were butter. After he rinsed the residue from his face, he applied a little bay rum shaving lotion. Then he preened in front of the mirror.

"This blacksmith cleans up pretty good, if I do say so myself."

The happy melody was still playing in his head when August dismounted in front of the house. Since it was already noon, he decided to tie the horse to the hitching post and take it to the barn after he ate. When the door opened following his rap on it, August stood and stared.

He saw a vision of loveliness framed in the doorway. Anna. She was wearing a green dress that brought out the highlights in her hazel eyes. This was the first time he had seen her in anything but black since the funeral. Actually, this was the first time he had seen her at all. She hadn't come to church or to town that he knew of, at least not in the last two weeks. He had heard from Gerda that Anna hardly left her room. What was she doing here?

❧

Anna didn't know that they were expecting August to eat with them. When the knock sounded on the door, she thought it might be one of their many customers. The dressmaking business thrived. She opened the door to see if she could help, instead of bothering Gerda or Olina.

Although she was tall, she had to look up into the face of the man standing there. August. He was wearing a blue plaid shirt that made his eyes seem more blue than gray. He looked fresh and clean, his face newly shaven. For an instant, she wanted to test the smoothness with her fingertips.

What was wrong with her? This was August. Gerda's brother. The strong, shy, quiet Nilsson brother. Then a snippet of a thought flitted through her mind. A phrase that Merta had uttered when they had been working on her wedding dress. Something about August being interested in Anna. For some reason, he had captured her gaze, and she caught a glimpse of something she couldn't define.

"Are you two going to stand there gaping at each other, or are you going to invite my brother in?" Gerda came up behind Anna. "Dinner is on the table. You're just in time."

Gerda took August by the arm and led him to the table. Anna gave her head a slight shake to clear her thoughts and followed her friends.

❧

Mrs. Braxton ordered three new dresses for the upcoming holiday season. And Marja wasn't a patient person. She was anxious to get the garments, even though it was still over a week before Thanksgiving.

Normally Anna used the sewing machine, stitching up the

major seams of the designs. When she finished each dress, Gerda did the handwork and added the decorations. But today Gerda wasn't in the sunny workroom. She had gone to town. August wanted her to help him bring something to the house. Probably for Gustaf or Olina.

Ever since Anna started working with Gerda, August was always underfoot. If he wasn't helping Gustaf with some repair on the house, he was running errands or doing other things for Gerda. Didn't that man have a job of his own that he needed to see about?

The thought wasn't fair, and Anna knew it. August was a hard worker. Mr. Simpkins had employed him for several years. Recently, Mr. Simpkins decided to retire and move to California where his daughter and her family lived. August had saved enough money to buy him out, so he did. Now he was the only blacksmith in town. That kept him plenty busy.

Maybe he didn't have much of a social life, since he spent so much time over here. Anna laughed. Who was she to comment on the social life of others? Hers consisted of eating dinner with her family and working with Gerda. Sometimes she took a break and played with Olga so Olina could get some rest. But that was the extent of her activities. Of course, that wasn't a bad thing. Since she started working here, she could relegate to the dark recesses of her mind all the events that had plagued her while she was holed up in her room for those two weeks. Thoughts she didn't want to entertain, but that never actually left her for long.

Anna finished stitching the skirt to the bodice of the dress. When she lifted the garment and repositioned it, the material filled her lap. She hoped she wouldn't crush it too badly.

"Oh good, you're finished." Gerda breezed into the room

from the door that opened onto the front porch. "I wanted to try this out."

Anna looked past Gerda to see August enter carrying something that was wrapped in brown paper. Legs stuck out from the paper, two at one end and one near the other end of the contraption.

"What's that?" Anna stood and folded the dress over the back of the chair where she had been sitting.

"It's an ironing table." Gerda smiled up at her brother. "August built it for us. Now we don't have to clear off the cutting table to iron something."

August pulled off the paper that had protected the top. It was long and thin with padding tied around it. He had even tapered one end to make it easier to slip items on it.

Anna glanced over at the potbellied stove where their irons rested when not in use. "Maybe we should set it near the stove. That way we won't have to carry the flatirons so far."

"Good idea." August moved the contraption and situated it a comfortable distance from the irons. "How's this?"

Anna thought he was asking Gerda, but he turned questioning eyes toward her. "It looks fine to me." She picked up the dress she had been working on. "I'll try it out."

After laying the garment on the new addition to the workroom, she picked up one of the flatirons, using the thick pad of fabric they kept nearby to protect their hands from the heat of the iron handle. While she applied heated pressure to the dress, she peeked at August, who was carrying on a conversation with Gerda.

Why hadn't she ever noticed how handsome he was? He was so quiet he didn't draw attention to himself. The work he did helped him develop extremely muscular arms and chest. His shirt stretched tight over them whenever he moved.

Anna almost wished he had been the one who had sought her out first. With his gentle nature, he probably wouldn't have broken her heart the way Gustaf and Olaf had. What was she thinking? Here she was still mourning the loss of Olaf. How could she compare him to another man?

❧

All the time August talked to Gerda, he was aware of every move Anna made. As she bent over the ironing table and pressed the heavy, hot iron into the fabric, he hoped she wouldn't burn herself. He knew it was impossible not to get burned occasionally when you used one of those. He remembered many times Gerda, and even his mother, had to deal with a blister on their hands or arms from ironing.

A war raged within him every time he came to this house and found Anna here. When he looked at her, all the longing he felt for her from the first time he saw her surged to the surface. Along with it came the fierce jealousy. Jealousy of Gustaf for capturing her heart before he tried. Even jealousy of a dead man for the time he had held her heart in his hands. Why couldn't he get past this jealousy? Maybe some day he would be able to think of Anna as something more than his brother's castoff. But not yet. Not today.

❧

Anna thought she had gotten used to August's appearance at the Nilsson house, but it always startled her. She had moved the sewing machine in front of the window so the sunlight would help her see what she was doing. While she concentrated on keeping the gathers even as she sewed a ruffle onto the skirt of one of the dresses for Mrs. Braxton, she became aware of a wagon stopping in front of the house. She hoped it wasn't Marja coming for the dresses. They weren't quite ready.

When she finished the seam, she looked up, and there he

was mounting the front steps. Today August didn't look like a blacksmith. Anna had never seen him in buckskins before. If she hadn't known better, she would have thought he was a trapper. If he quit shaving, he would have made a good mountain man with blond whiskers and strong muscles under the leather clothing. She had never been drawn to those untamed men when they came into town. They were often unwashed and smelly. Anna knew that August usually smelled faintly of bay rum shaving lotion. For a moment, she could imagine those strong leather-clad arms holding her—

"Who is that?" Gerda asked from her place by the ironing table. "I can't see from here."

Anna was glad that Gerda interrupted her crazy thoughts. "It's August." She stood up, placed her fists against her waist, and stretched her back. She had been sitting at the sewing machine too long without moving. "What's he doing here? He didn't come for lunch, did he? I thought we were going to eat sandwiches made from yesterday's leftovers for our noon meal."

Gerda placed the iron back on the stove and went toward the door. "We are. But it's too early for lunch. I think he's going hunting. He said that his contribution to the community Thanksgiving dinner would be a deer, since he doesn't cook."

Hunting? August is going hunting? Fear clutched Anna in a tight grip. Her heart ached. Something of what she felt must have shown on her face when Gerda turned toward her.

"Anna, what's the matter? You're white as a sheet."

"Nothing." Anna reached for the back of the straight chair where she had been sitting. Now she felt dread, but not the uncanny dread she had felt when Olaf left to go on his last hunting trip. Would she always feel this way when someone she knew went hunting? Surely not.

Gerda came and put her arm around Anna. "Have you

been working too long? Maybe we should take a break."

August knocked on the door of the workroom instead of the door to the rest of the house. Gerda quickly went to let him in.

❧

When Gerda opened the door, August looked past her to where Anna leaned on the back of a chair. Sunlight streamed through the window and bathed her in a golden glow that should have gilded her beauty. Instead she looked frail, almost as if something was wrong with her. He wondered what it was. He had always thought of Anna as strong. That was one of the things he loved about her, her strength. But she didn't look strong today.

"Come in." Gerda stepped back to make room for him. "We were just going to take a break. Do you have time for a cup of coffee with us before you go?"

August looked from Anna's pale face to Gerda's cheerful one. "Sounds good, for sure. The wind has a bite in it today. This trip could be a cold one. Wouldn't hurt to warm up first."

Gerda put her arm around his waist as they started toward the kitchen. "So what really brought you over here?"

August glanced back at Anna. He was going to stop Gerda, but Anna had turned to follow them. "Gustaf said I could use his new rifle. It's more accurate than mine, and I don't want to stay out in the cold any longer than I have to."

❧

Anna was glad to hear August's last statement. It made her feel better, but not much. She followed them into the kitchen.

"Where is Olina?" August looked around the warm room.

"She took Olga to see her grandmother."

Anna picked up the coffeepot that sat on the back of the cookstove, poured August a mugful, and set it on the table in front of him. Then she poured hot water into a teapot and set tea to steep. Gerda uncovered a pan of cinnamon rolls that were left from breakfast.

"I would have come over sooner if I had known you had cinnamon rolls." August forked two onto the plate Gerda set in front of him.

"How long will you be gone?" Anna kept her back to the table. She didn't want anyone to know how important his answer was to her.

When he didn't answer, she turned around. No wonder. He was chewing the big bite that was missing from one of the rolls in front of him. Always the gentleman, he wouldn't talk with his mouth full.

"As soon as I see a large deer and kill it, I'll field dress it and return to town." He took a swig of the hot coffee.

Anna wondered how he could drink it so fast. She always let her tea cool off a bit before she sipped it.

"There's a storm brewing, and I don't want to be out in it too long. Maybe it'll only snow this time."

Anna could imagine him huddled in the cold. She didn't welcome this feeling of sympathy for him. She didn't want to feel anything for any man. Her life would be much more uncomplicated without men.

August had been gone barely half an hour when feathery flakes started floating past the window. Could it have been only an hour before that sunlight poured through the same window? Where was August now? Where would he camp? Did he have plenty of warm clothes? Could he find enough dry wood for his campfire? Why did he have to go hunting alone? Anna wished the questions wouldn't dance through her mind, taunting her. She could hardly wait until August came back, hopefully driving his own wagon.

four

Not a day had gone by since August left that Anna didn't hope to hear his wagon come to the house. At least the storm had only held snow. Although several inches covered the ground, the air hadn't warmed up enough to thaw any of it, so there wasn't much ice. Anna knew that August was a careful hunter. He was skilled at making camp and building a fire—all the things that were needed to be successful. But the longer he was gone, the more her mind filled with pictures of the day Olaf had returned in the bed of the wagon. And August didn't have anyone with him to bring him home.

Why did she care? It seemed as if Anna asked herself that question a million times. August was just a friend, but he was a good friend. Her best friend's brother. Anyone would care under those circumstances. Why did her concern feel like much more than that?

Gustaf went out to the farm one morning, leaving Olina and Olga with Anna and Gerda. Olina was having a hard day, and Olga was full of energy. She had been inside for the last week. Gerda bundled Olga up in several layers of clothing and took her outside to play in the snow. Anna decided to stay indoors and work on one of the many dresses clients had ordered. That way she could keep a discreet watch on Olina.

Anna liked the fabric for the new outfit. It was a rich mulberry wool with a soft touch. As Anna smoothed the fabric out across the top of the cutting table, she imagined herself in a suit from the dark purple fabric. A fitted jacket with a short peplum spreading over a full skirt. She would line the jacket with lavender silk. A blouse of the same silk with a froth of ruffles to fill the V neckline. Even with the blouse, the suit would be dark enough for someone who had lost her fiancé to death. Maybe she should leave work early enough today to go by the mercantile and purchase the fabric on her way home. She didn't want the store to sell out before she got some.

The sound of hoofbeats mingled with the shouts of laughter coming from the yard. Anna glanced out the window. It was just Gustaf returning home. She looked back at the piece of paper containing the customer's measurements. Then she realized what else she had seen. Gustaf was carrying his rifle. The rifle August had taken hunting with him.

Anna couldn't have stopped herself from going to the window if she had tried. She wanted to be sure. Gustaf tied the horse to the hitching post and started up the sidewalk to the house, and he carried the rifle. Anna didn't realize that she was holding her breath until she released it. Why did she feel as if a heavy load had been lifted from her shoulders? She didn't want to look at the answer to that question.

Anna had made the first slice through the fabric with her scissors when Gerda and Olga tumbled through the door. Gerda set Olga in a corner near the window and gave her a bucket of wooden spools to play with.

"So why did Gustaf come home early?" Anna tried to sound disinterested, but she knew she failed.

Gerda came over to watch. "He wanted to talk to Olina." She fingered an edge of the fabric. "I like the feel of this wool, don't you?"

Anna nodded while she continued cutting. "I thought I saw him carrying the rifle August borrowed." Anna didn't look up from her work. She didn't want Gerda to see how relieved she was.

"Yes, August arrived at our house a few minutes before Gustaf left the farm to come home." Gerda turned and leaned against the end of the table. "He brought two deer. I think Gustaf wants Olina and Olga to go out to the farm with him. They're probably going to spend the night."

Anna pulled the blades of the scissors away from the fabric to protect it and looked at Gerda. "Why would they do that?"

"Have you forgotten what tomorrow is?"

Tomorrow? Thursday. "Thanksgiving." Anna had tried to put it out of her mind. She wasn't looking forward to all the celebrating.

"It'll take all afternoon to process the meat." Gerda started picking up and putting away all the things that were out of place in the room. "One deer will be kept for our family's meals, and the other will be roasted for the community Thanksgiving dinner. It'll take all night. Far and August are building the fire in the pit Gustaf dug. The fire'll have to burn down to coals before they put the deer in it."

Anna laid the scissors on the table, being careful to close the blades so there wouldn't be a mishap. "Are you going with them?"

Gerda nodded. "Yes. The whole family will be preparing for the big feast."

"I can finish this Monday." Anna started to put on her coat and scarf. "I want to stop at the mercantile on the way home anyway."

❧

When August arrived at the community center for the Thanksgiving shindig, he immediately started looking for Anna. If she came, it would be the first event she had attended since the funeral. Because she hadn't started coming to church again, he was afraid she wouldn't be here either. He decided that if she didn't come, he would take food to her house for her.

He came early with his mother and sister to help set everything up. Gustaf and his father would bring Olina and Olga when they brought the roasted deer meat right before noon.

While Gerda swept the floor, August helped set up tables across one wall of the large room. Then he placed chairs all around the other three sides. Each time he passed a window, he glanced toward the road that led to the Jenson horse farm. And each time, the road was empty, making his heart grow heavier and heavier.

After they had worked for a couple of hours, the room looked festive. Gerda and Mother had a knack for decorating. All that was missing was the food that would soon cover the tables. The sound of a buggy coming down the road drew August to the window, but it wasn't the Jenson buggy.

Other vehicles joined the first in rapid succession. People filled the tables with food and the room with merriment as they greeted neighbors and caught up on recent activities. August leaned one shoulder against the back wall and watched everyone. He didn't feel much like socializing. Besides, no one would probably notice if he wasn't there. He wasn't exactly the life of the party. He wasn't sure anyone would even be aware if he walked out the door and didn't return.

He decided to try out his theory, but before he reached the door, it burst open. Lowell and Ollie Jenson carried in baskets laden with food. Behind them, Mrs. Jenson was talking to Anna as they entered the warm building. The temperature had risen above freezing and started melting the snow, but there was still a chill in the air.

August sat in one of the chairs by the wall and crossed his

ankle over his other knee. He leaned the chair back against the wall and tried to act nonchalant. Of course, if his mother saw him, she would probably come tell him to sit with all four legs of the chair on the floor. She wouldn't care that he was an adult who'd been living on his own for several years. He decided not to tempt her, so he uncrossed his legs, dropped the chair back down, and leaned his elbows on his knees. With his hands dangling between his long legs, he watched Anna as she sidled up to the table and made sure her brothers had put each dish in the proper place.

Anna had a look like a lost little girl. She glanced around the room and moved toward a back corner. August knew that she hadn't wanted to come. He got up and followed her.

"I'm glad you're here, Anna."

❧

The sound of her name startled Anna. She turned around and looked at the top button of August's shirt. Where had he come from? She hadn't noticed him in any of the clusters of men she passed. What was he doing standing so close to her? For some reason, she liked the way he said her name. She'd heard him say it many times before, but somehow it sounded different today.

"I almost didn't." Anna lifted her gaze to his face.

Today August wasn't wearing buckskins, but he looked every bit as virile without them. His denim trousers were new, and his shirt was a blue that brought out the color of his eyes. Anna was close enough to step into his arms. She shifted back to give herself some space and took a deep breath. Mingled with the tantalizing scents of food that permeated the air was the distinctive aroma of bay rum shaving lotion. This was only August, Gerda's brother. Why was his presence crowding her, even though he stood a couple of feet away?

Anna decided that her emotions were too raw. She had told Mother that she wasn't ready to be in a crowd, and she must have been right.

When Anna arrived home that evening, she was tired, but it was a good tired. The day had gone better than she hoped. No one asked her about Olaf. People seemed to understand that she didn't want to talk about what had happened. The women drew her into several conversations. The most prominent subject was the clothing that she and Gerda had been producing in their workroom. Several of the women wore garments with their distinctive touches. Those conversations helped Anna relax. Before the day was over, other women mentioned that they were going to stop by the shop and talk about holiday dresses. It looked as if she and Gerda would have their hands full, at least for the next month. And that was a good thing.

The only uncomfortable times Anna experienced were when she was too close to August. Her long-time friend had grown into a strong, handsome man. Were all the other young single women blind? He should've had plenty of feminine attention. That would've kept him from seeking her out every chance he got. Or so it seemed to her.

Anna was sure that August only felt sorry for her. He couldn't have been feeling anything else. But his presence made her uncomfortable. She didn't need this. Didn't he realize that there was something wrong with her? That some strange phenomenon kept a man from loving her enough? That fact had been amply demonstrated in the past. Gustaf had seemed ready to ask her to marry him before Olina arrived. But that changed fast enough. And Olaf had loved her in his own way, she supposed. But it was a lukewarm love at best. Her feelings and desires hadn't meant much to him, had they? If they had, she would be married right now.

Well, she wasn't going to put herself through that agony again. Her life was full with friends and her work. That's all she needed. Wasn't it? She would never marry. That was for sure.

❧

The day after Thanksgiving, August was back at work. The heat from the forge staved off the chill from outside. He was even able to leave the door open without the room getting too cold. He added more fuel to the fire, then turned to look at all the items that needed repairing. They were lined up on one table in the order in which he had received them. A testimony to his hard work. Anna's brothers would be here any minute with several horses that needed shoeing. He'd get back to the other things after they left.

Every time August turned around, he was reminded of Anna. Beautiful Anna. He couldn't take his eyes off her yesterday. She wasn't wearing one of the brighter colors she favored before she lost Olaf, but the warm brown of her suit brought out the rich darkness of her eyes. August liked the way her eyes changed color according to what she wore. Although she had her hair pulled into a figure-eight bun fastened at her neck, she looked soft and feminine. August was disgusted that he hadn't taken his chance when he had it. She should be loved, not mourning a loss.

These thoughts brought him full circle to the jealousy he had to fight all the time. If he had been less shy, he would have spoken to her before Gustaf did. Now look at him. He didn't know if he would ever marry. She was the one woman he could love. But not now.

August picked up an iron bar and held it in the flame of the forge. After it was red hot, he placed it on the anvil and bent it into a horseshoe shape. The pounding didn't work out his tension as it usually did. He held the bar back in the fire to reheat so he could pound it flat. When that was accomplished, he plunged it into the tub of cold water that sputtered and spit as it cooled the finished product.

It took almost an hour to form as many horseshoes as he thought he would need. When he laid the last one on the bench, Ollie and Lowell rode up to the door. Each one led two horses behind their own mounts.

❧

Gerda was already hard at work when Anna arrived at the workroom on Monday morning. She watched as Anna took off her coat and hung it up.

"So, what are you working on?" Anna moved toward the table. "I think I'll finish cutting this out."

"Okay." Gerda held up the waistband of the skirt she was hemming. "I just now finished this. It's a good thing. Mrs. Larkin is coming to pick it up this morning."

Anna picked up her scissors and bent over the fabric for the suit, which was still spread across the table. She slid the scissors back into the place where she had stopped cutting the day before Thanksgiving. Carefully, she followed the outlines she had drawn on the fabric.

Gerda stood and started folding the skirt. "I was glad you came to church yesterday. We have missed you there."

Anna continued cutting. "I know, and I missed being there." She reached the end of the long side of the skirt, so she had to turn the scissors a different direction. She moved around the edge of the table so her hand wasn't at an uncomfortable angle to cut the rest of the garment. "It wasn't as bad as I thought it would be."

"Bad?" Gerda stopped folding and walked over to Anna. "Why would going to church be bad?"

Anna carefully laid the scissors down and stood up, looking her friend in the eye. "I thought that everyone would be sympathetic. . .or ask questions or something."

Gerda smiled. "Oh, Anna. Everyone cares about you, but no one wants to make you uncomfortable."

"I know that. And it helps."

Olina knocked on the door that connected to the parlor, then opened it. "I want to talk to you two."

Anna pulled up a chair and offered it to Olina. Then she sat on a stool that was beside the cutting table.

"What's on your mind?" Gerda picked up the folded skirt and placed it on the shelf where the finished articles were kept.

"Now that Thanksgiving is over, we need to think about Christmas."

"Isn't it a little early?" Anna asked.

"Not at all." Olina leaned forward as if she were eager. "I love Christmas."

Anna nodded. "I always have, too."

Olina looked up at her. "I know that you have your own family, but I really need help here. That buggy ride out to the farm gets harder and harder. I would like to have Christmas for the family here at our house, but I can't do it by myself. Would you two help me?"

Anna thought a minute. "I might have to spend Christmas Day at home with my family, but I could help you prepare. That is, if you give us time to work on all the orders we have."

Olina clapped her hands. It reminded Anna of the way Marja Braxton at the mercantile always clapped her hands when she was excited. Maybe Olina was picking up some of her habits.

"August said he would help us, too."

When Anna started home, riding on Buttermilk, she revisited

the conversation with Olina. Did Anna really want to spend that much time with August? It might not be too bad. . .if she could remember that he was only a friend. She wondered why she was thinking so much about him. She was supposed to have been in love with Olaf, and it had only been a couple of months since he died. She should still feel devastated, shouldn't she?

She had been so upset when Gustaf turned away from her love for him. Wasn't she turning away from her love of Olaf in the same way?

A thought struck Anna in the heart. Maybe she hadn't loved Olaf any more than he loved her. Was she truly in love with him, or was she only in love with the idea of being a wife and mother? Anna didn't like what she saw deep inside her heart.

She had liked Olaf. A lot. They had fun together, but something was missing from their relationship. Up until now, she had felt that the lack was one sided. Only Olaf didn't express the love she needed. Maybe the reason he didn't love her enough was because she didn't really love him either. Perhaps on some level, he understood that. It could be that the love they felt for each other wasn't strong enough to carry them through all the stresses of married life. Maybe God hadn't wanted her to marry Olaf. Maybe He didn't want her to be married at all.

Why is life so complicated?

Anna pushed aside these thoughts and put her mind to the plans for Christmas. That was what she needed. Something to keep her busy.

Anna felt that she reached a turning point during that ride home. She was strong. An independent business-woman. Her life was full. She didn't need anything else. Especially not a man.

five

January 1895

As Anna drove the buggy toward the dress shop, her thoughts returned to Christmas. Not only did she spend holiday time with her own family, she had been included in the festivities at the Nilssons'. Since most of their celebrations took place at Gustaf and Olina's house, and since Olina needed Gerda and Anna to help her, Anna's time had been completely filled. She knew that if she had had much time to think, she would have had a hard time with the holiday. As it was, she was able to close off her heart from the pain and fill her life with the busyness Christmas brought to her.

Another benefit of her activities was the fact that she felt competent. While she was helping with all the cooking, decorating, and gift preparation, her confidence grew. More and more, the idea of her independence blossomed within her. Any doubts or lingering desires for a marriage and children were quickly pushed into some far recess of her mind. She made a concerted effort to forget that they were there.

During the holidays, Olina had talked to Gerda and Anna. She wanted Anna to take her place in the dressmaking business. Olina would have her hands full with her home and family. Anna had wondered how she and Gerda would continue to work, since they were using the room at Gustaf and Olina's house for a workroom. Olina told them that it was not an imposition, since Gerda was family anyway. Now

Anna was half owner of a successful business.

Although the remnants of the latest snowfall had turned mushy, Anna didn't have any problems getting to work that morning. She felt proud of herself as she drove the buggy through the open door of Gustaf's barn. She was so lost in her thoughts that she didn't wonder why the barn door was open on such a cold day.

"Anna, let me help you."

Almost before she could turn her head, two large hands rested on her waist and strong arms lifted her down from the conveyance. When she glanced up, she was standing much too close to August.

"What are you doing here?" She couldn't keep her question from sounding breathless.

"Aren't you glad to see me?"

The twinkle in his eyes reached a place dangerously near her heart. Anna took a couple of steps back, almost tumbling over the barn cat.

"I just didn't expect you to be here at this time of day."

She started removing her soft leather gloves. The sooner she got the horse into a stall, the better. Who knew how long August would be there?

The jingle of the harness caused Anna to look up from her hands. August was already leading the horse toward the stall she usually used. He grabbed a brush on the way.

"You don't have to do that."

August smiled back at her. "I know I don't, but I want to." He continued toward the stall.

Anna stood watching him as if she were dumbfounded. Why was he doing this? After a moment, she mumbled, "Thank you." Then she turned and hurried out of the barn as if something were chasing her.

When she was halfway to the house, she heard August give a hearty laugh followed by, "You're welcome."

What was so funny? She shook her head and rounded the side of the house. She wondered if Gerda had arrived. When she entered the workroom, she found a note telling her that Gerda had gone to the mercantile. It was a little early in the day for that, wasn't it? Without another thought, Anna turned her attention to the many garments that needed work. She thought that when the holidays were over, the orders would slow down. But it had been a good year, and that didn't happen. The more often women in the area wore their new dresses, the more orders she and Gerda received. Actually, they could use a larger workroom. If only that were possible.

"Anna!"

Gerda's exuberant greeting as she entered the front door startled Anna. She looked up from the gabardine skirt she was cutting out.

"Guess what!" Gerda threw off her navy wool cape, letting it slip to the floor, then started pulling off her knitted gloves.

Anna put the scissors on the table and turned to lean against it, crossing her arms. "I'm sure I don't know."

Gerda grabbed Anna and hugged her. "It's the most wonderful news."

Anna could hardly catch her breath because Gerda was hugging her so hard. "Well, tell me before you squeeze me in two."

Gerda pulled away and laughed. She walked over to the heavy laden shelves along the back wall of the workroom.

"See how crowded we are."

Anna nodded, hoping that Gerda would hurry and tell what was making her so excited.

"How would you like to have a larger workroom?"

Had she read Anna's mind? Anna turned, picked up the

scissors, and started cutting again. "That would be nice, but I'm sure that if Gustaf were to add a room to the house, it wouldn't be for us."

Gerda dropped onto the stool beside the cutting table. "That's not what I'm talking about." She leaned her elbows on the end of the table that wasn't covered with material. "When I was in town, the Braxtons asked if we would like to have a dress shop in the mercantile. They think it would help the store if we did. Johan even offered to give us space for a larger workroom as well as a display area. Both Johan and Marja think it will bring more customers into the store and increase their sales."

Anna had stopped cutting halfway through Gerda's explanation. She laid the scissors down and leaned back against the edge of the table, crossing her arms. "What did you tell them?"

"That I needed to talk to you. What do you think?"

Anna stood deep in thought. A dress shop in town. She could just picture a dress form in the front window featuring a beautiful outfit. Lace panels pulled back with cord ties gave a pleasing frame for the display. A real salesroom and a workroom, maybe room for storage.

She turned toward Gerda and smiled. "I like it. How would it work?"

Gerda stood and went to pick up her cape and gloves from where she dropped them. She hung the garment on a hook on the wall. "Remember when the Braxtons bought the building next door to the mercantile and expanded into it? They have been trying to update the merchandise they carry. It's the 1890s, and our city is growing. They want to be more modern. They think the dress shop would be a welcome addition to the mercantile. They would let us have a portion of the right side of the store. We would probably need to get our brothers to help with the remodeling we need to do, but we could have a salesroom with a workroom behind it. And the workroom would be twice as large as this one. Johan said that they would only charge us a small percentage of sales for rent."

"I like it. Let's do it." This only added to Anna's feeling of being an independent modern woman. Oh yes, she would have a fulfilling life as a successful businesswoman. And if Gerda ever decided to marry and have a family, then Anna would run the store by herself. Maybe this was what God had planned for her life all along. If it hadn't matched her plans for herself, that didn't matter. She took the new idea to heart, pushing everything else to the back of her mind.

❧

It was a good thing it was the middle of winter. Otherwise, Gerda and Anna wouldn't have had the help they needed to open the dress shop. Ollie and Lowell were glad to be working inside. So were Gustaf and August.

All four of the men showed up at the mercantile on Monday morning to start the renovation. Anna and Gerda arrived at about the same time as their brothers. Mr. Braxton quickly took them to the section he had set aside for the new venture.

Anna looked at the area that had been roped off. It was such a small part of the store, but even empty as it was now, it was so much larger than their workroom at Gustaf and Olina's house.

"I thought that we could put up a wall going from the front between the windows all the way to the back of the building." Mr. Braxton made a sweeping gesture with his arm. "It would mean taking down one wall, so you would have access that far back."

Anna was amazed. She had assumed that the dress shop would only extend to the wall that separated the store from the storeroom behind it. If he was going to let them have that area, too, they would have plenty of room to work and ample space for storage.

"Are you sure you want us to have all that space?" Anna asked Johan. She didn't want any misunderstandings. If she was going to be a successful businesswoman, she needed to start right now by taking care of every detail.

"Oh, yes." Johan nodded. "It will almost be as though you have your own separate store."

Gerda and Anna walked along the rope, looking at the empty space. Then they went into the storeroom to see how much more space was available to them. When they came back into the main part of the store, their brothers were making plans with Johan.

August looked toward the two young women. "I think we should ask Anna and Gerda exactly what they want."

"Of course," Johan agreed. "Gerda and Anna, how much of this space do you want for your salesroom and how much for the workroom?"

Gerda and Anna looked at each other. Anna wondered if they knew what they were getting themselves into. There were so many decisions to make.

"Why don't we get started on taking the wall to the storeroom down? That would give them some time to discuss what they want." August picked up a hammer and saw, then started toward the back wall. The other men followed him.

Anna was glad she had thought to bring a pencil and some paper. She and Gerda stood beside one of the empty counters and started discussing what they wanted, drawing it on the paper. It took about an hour, but they agreed about what was needed.

Anna walked toward the hardworking men with confidence, while Gerda went to the front of the store to look at the windows. The excitement of the day had reinforced Anna's determination to become a very successful shopkeeper. She started to show her drawings to her brothers. August, Gustaf, and Johan noticed and joined them.

"We would like a wall that goes all the way from the front to the back of the building, with a door from the mercantile into the display area and a door from the storeroom of the mercantile into our storage area. The only entrances into the workroom will be from the salesroom and the storeroom."

After showing the men the drawings she and Gerda had made, Anna walked over to the place where the wall between the display area and working space should be. With a defining gesture, she marked the exact line where it would be placed. Gustaf took a piece of chalk from his pocket and drew a line on the floor. Turning, Anna marched through the hole the men had made in the wall.

"We don't need as much area for storage as you do, Mr. Braxton, so we want our other wall right here." Anna used her right hand to slice through the air in the exact spot.

Once again, Gustaf used the chalk to mark the place.

❧

August watched Anna as she gave directions to the men. A different Anna had emerged today. An Anna who was strong, in command of the situation. Who even showed a slightly hard edge. He wasn't sure he liked that. No longer could he see the sparkle that usually lit her eyes. During the holidays, it had finally started coming back, but now it looked as if it had been entirely extinguished. She had been more and more like the old Anna he had fallen in love with so many years ago. Suddenly, that Anna had once again disappeared to be replaced by this stranger. This. . .businesswoman.

Even though a new century was fast approaching, August

wasn't sure he agreed with the modern women he saw emerging all around him. He wanted women to be like his mother. A homemaker, wife, and mother whose main focus was her family. Not a shopkeeper who ran a successful business. If a woman needed to work, that was one thing, but couldn't she keep some of the more desirable qualities?

"Hey, Brother, are you going to help us, or are you going to stand there and stare?" Gustaf interrupted his thought process.

August turned around and walked toward the remnants of the wall they were removing. Only a little more work, and they could start building the new walls.

❧

On Tuesday, Gerda and Anna designed the workroom, while the men built the long wall that would divide their shop from the mercantile. They drew the plan for shelves and tables that would make their work easier. Of course, they would be able to bring most of the things they had been using at Gustaf and Olina's house. All except the built-in shelves. They had enough work to keep all four brothers busy for a couple of weeks, maybe longer.

"Anna." Mr. Braxton spoke only to her, as if he, too, recognized that she was in charge. "I have ordered a new sign for over the mercantile. Have you ever met Silas Johnson?" When Anna shook her head, he continued. "He's a painter who moved to town about six months ago. His fancy lettering made him an instant hit with the merchants. He's doing our sign. Do you want a separate sign from the mercantile?"

Gerda had been listening to the conversation. She turned to Anna. "That would be good, but we need to decide what to name our part of the store. Do you have any ideas?"

Anna thought for a minute. "What about the Dress Emporium?"

"Oh, I like that. Wouldn't it be wonderful if we could have the letters painted on the glass?" Gerda started doodling on the tablet they were using for their plans. "Maybe in an arc like this." She printed block letters on the paper to illustrate what she meant. "But with the same kind of fancy letters that the Braxtons are using for the mercantile."

Marja had been stocking shelves a little way from where her husband was talking to their new tenants, so she had heard the conversation. "That would really give both stores an elegant look, wouldn't it." She clapped her hands as she usually did when she was excited. "We'll have the painter do both at the same time."

❧

It had taken three weeks for the Dress Emporium to be finished. While the men worked at the store, Gerda and Anna stayed in the workroom at Gustaf and Olina's house. There were too many orders from customers for them to take three weeks off. But every day they both went to check on the progress of their new space.

One day when Anna stepped into the mercantile, August met her. "I think you need some windows in the work area."

For a moment, Anna was lost in his intent gaze.

"They will give you much more light to work by."

"Yes. . .that's a good idea." She stepped back to give herself breathing space.

The next time Anna went to the store, she was amazed at the amount of light they had in the workroom. The men had put three windows on the outside wall. She was touched by August's thoughtfulness in making the suggestion.

As she returned to the Nilsson home, she started planning in her head where they should put the stove, the Singer sewing machine, the ironing table, and the cutting table.

There was so much room. It was a real blessing.

The men finished their work on Thursday, so everyone planned to help Anna and Gerda move in on Friday. That way the first day of business would be Saturday, when many of the people from outlying farms came into town to shop.

"What are we going to display in the window?" Gerda came through the door carrying a basket with sewing notions in it. "We need something to catch people's attention."

Anna glanced at the dress form she was taking to the workroom. Then she looked at the big window in the front of the store. An idea began to form in her mind. Why not?

"I'll take care of the window." Anna turned toward Gerda. "You set up the rest of the salesroom. I have to go home for something." With that, Anna strode from the building and mounted her mare that was tied to the hitching post in front of the mercantile.

With determination, she rode toward home, her head buzzing with plans. Before long she returned to the store, driving a wagon with a trunk in the back.

❧

August came out of the store when she stopped the wagon. "Do you need help with that trunk?" He liked the way Anna looked. The cold breeze had put a lot of color in her cheeks. "I'll get it for you." After August hefted the trunk onto his broad shoulders, he started toward the door of the dress shop. "Where do you want it?"

Anna hurried to keep up with him. "In the workroom. Over in the empty corner. I'll take care of it from there."

August could tell that she was excited about something. He wondered what it was. He wished he had time to just look at her, but there was still a lot that needed his attention. How could he have ever let his jealousy keep him from trying to establish a romantic relationship with Anna? Now her whole attention was being poured into this store. Would there ever be room in her life for him? Had he waited too long?

six

"What are you doing?"

Gerda's loud entrance startled Anna. She looked up from the dress she was pressing to where Gerda stood in the doorway with her arms full of packages.

"Is that your. . .?" Gerda looked troubled.

"Yes, it's my wedding dress." Anna returned the flatiron to the stove and picked up another one.

Gerda came into the room and dropped the packages on the table that sat in the middle of the room. "Why are you pressing your wedding dress?"

Anna remained intent on her task, pushing the heated iron carefully across the cloth that covered the delicate silk. Although most brides wore other colors, she had followed the example of the English Queen Victoria and chosen white.

"I won't ever wear this dress."

Gerda didn't pick up on Anna's meaning. "Because you didn't marry Olaf doesn't mean you won't ever get married. But what are you going to do with it?"

Anna placed the cooling flatiron back on the stove and exchanged it for one that was ready to be used, ignoring Gerda's first comment. "It will make a wonderful display. I'm going to put it on the dress form in the window. With the lace curtains you and Marja picked out, it should draw attention to the store."

After once again placing the flatiron on the stove, Anna carefully picked up the dress and carried it into the salesroom without wrinkling it. She gently laid it on the counter, then went to the window and pulled the form back a little.

Gerda followed. "What if someone wants to buy it?"

Anna stopped what she was doing and thought a moment. "Then I guess we'll sell it. . . That's what we're in business for, to make money." She gathered up the dress and started fitting it on the form. "What do you have in those packages you brought in?" Anna hoped to take Gerda's attention off the wedding dress, and it worked.

"I'll show you." Gerda went into the other room and returned with two of the packages.

She dropped them on the counter and started untying the string around one. When she pulled back the brown paper, handmade crocheted items spilled out.

"Olina thought we could sell these in the shop. She crochets when Olga takes a nap." Gerda picked up a pair of lacy gloves. "We can put these things on the counter or a shelf right now. Maybe we could bring in a highboy or some small tables to place around the room. Then we could display these and other accessories to go with the dresses women order from us."

Anna finished placing the form with the wedding dress in the center of the window. Then she came over to look at what Gerda had. "That's a good idea, and it'll help Olina, since she doesn't feel like working in the shop."

While Anna started arranging the items from the first two packages, Gerda retrieved the others from the workroom. When they had everything displayed to their satisfaction, both women turned around and surveyed the shop.

"This looks good." Anna stood with her arms crossed.

"Yes," Gerda agreed, "I think we're ready for business tomorrow."

"Not quite," Marja said, from the doorway to the mercantile.

"We have something for you."

When Gerda and Anna turned, they saw Johan carrying in a lovely screen decorated with a hand-painted still life made up of many soft colors of roses.

"What lovely flowers!" Gerda walked over to Johan and leaned over to examine them more closely.

Anna joined her. "I don't think I've ever seen a more lovely screen."

"When the women come for fittings, they can change clothes behind it." Marja smiled at them.

Anna straightened up and turned to Marja. "You don't mean this screen is for us?"

"Yes." Marja folded her hands in front of her waist.

Anna thought about the cost of such a screen. "We could pay you for it. We were planning on buying one later."

Marja shook her head. "No, it's our little gift for your new store."

"Where do you want it?" Johan asked.

Gerda and Anna looked at each other. "The workroom," they said in unison.

They followed Johan, and Anna showed him the corner where the screen should be placed. He unfolded the four panels and arranged it across the corner Anna indicated. It was over five feet tall, so it made a wonderful, private place, and the pretty flowers were a welcome addition to the room.

"Now." Marja clapped her hands. "You're ready for business."

❧

Several people brought tools to the blacksmith shop to be repaired. And most of them wanted theirs fixed before they returned to their farms late in the afternoon. So August was busy. He was glad. With all the time he had spent helping Anna and Gerda with the dress shop, he welcomed the income from the repairs. But while he was working on these things, his mind was half on his work and half on the new store on Main Street. He couldn't help wondering how potential shoppers were accepting the Dress Emporium.

August knew it looked good, even though he hadn't been back after helping Gerda and Anna move in the larger items. He wondered what changes they had made to turn it into the store they wanted it to be.

When August was finally finished with all the work, he went to clean up, even taking a bath and shaving. Usually, he waited to shave on Sunday morning before going to church. Maybe it wouldn't hurt his face too much to be shaved late in the afternoon and then the next morning, too.

As he walked down the sidewalk with his boots sounding a drumbeat on the wood, August was surprised to see what was in the window of the Dress Emporium. Usually he didn't pay that much attention to women's fashions, but he knew instinctively that it was a wedding dress. He stopped and admired the intricate lacy designs scattered over filmy material. He knew that the only thing that would have made the dress more beautiful would have been if Anna was wearing it. Wearing it and walking down the aisle of the church. Walking down the aisle of the church to meet him. His heart started beating the speed of the clacking wheels on the steam engine of a train that was pulling into town. He hoped he wasn't just torturing himself with these thoughts.

August pushed open the door to the Dress Emporium. "So who's getting married? I didn't hear about any weddings coming up."

Anna looked up from folding several pieces of fabric on the counter. "August, come in and shut the door. It's hard to keep the shop warm on a cold day like today."

Gerda didn't ignore his question. "No one we know is getting married soon."

August looked from his sister to Anna. "Then whose wedding dress is in the window?"

When Anna gasped, August wondered why. His strong gaze held her captive for a moment that stretched into an eon.

Finally, Gerda blurted, "It's Anna's."

When she did, something flickered in Anna's eyes. Something August didn't understand. Why was she selling her wedding dress? Anna tore her gaze from his and dropped hers to the items on the counter.

Gerda must have felt the uncomfortable silence, because she tried to fill it. "It's the dress we made for Anna to wear when she was going to marry Olaf." The statement ended almost in a whisper.

August turned to stare at the dress for a moment.

"I didn't know," he murmured, then glanced toward Anna. "I'm sorry I brought it up."

Anna turned to replace the folded fabric on the shelves behind the counter. "It's okay. I knew that everyone would see it when I put it in the window."

August walked over to the counter and leaned across it toward Anna. "Why are you selling the dress?"

Anna didn't turn around. She stood with one hand on the bolt of fabric so long that August thought she wasn't going to answer his question.

"I'll never wear it."

August wasn't sure what Anna meant, but he didn't like the way it sounded. So final. Emotions roiled within him. Emotions he couldn't even name. Why hadn't Anna turned toward him to answer? Was he making her uncomfortable? That wasn't what he wanted to do.

He moved back from the counter and looked around him. "I really like what you've done with the store."

Anna turned around, and Gerda hurried over to hug him. "Thanks, August."

"Have you had many customers?" He was talking to Gerda, but he couldn't keep from glancing at Anna out of the corner of his eyes. For a moment their gazes met, then Anna turned and went into the workroom.

Gerda looked toward the doorway where Anna had disappeared. "Yes, a lot of people stopped in to see the store. We have several orders for dresses, and we even sold some of the gloves and scarves that Olina crocheted."

August laughed. "It sounds as if you had a good day. I came to take you and Anna to the hotel for dinner."

"I'll ask her."

While Gerda was in the workroom, August moved to the wedding dress and looked at it more closely. If his hands hadn't been so rough, he would have touched its softness. He should have realized that it was Anna's. Not many women in town were that tall. He still wanted to see Anna wearing the dress. It would set off her dark beauty.

When Gerda and Anna returned from the workroom, August couldn't catch a glimpse of the Anna of a few minutes before. She had once again turned into the modern businesswoman who had emerged the last three weeks.

❧

On Monday, Gerda and Anna arrived at the shop at the same time. Immediately, they set to work on the orders they needed to finish right away. Before long, Marja breezed into the workroom.

"I have an idea." Her clap indicated that she was excited about it. "We need to plan a special opening celebration for the Dress Emporium."

Gerda looked up from the handwork she was doing. "But we're already open."

"Oh, the special opening doesn't have to be the first day of business." Marja nodded for emphasis. "We were open two weeks before we had our special opening. You can make sure that everything is all right with your store, and you have enough time to let people know to come."

Anna turned from the machine where she was sewing the seams of a blouse. "What do you do for this opening?"

Marja sat on a trunk that was near the cutting table. "When we had ours, we had posters printed and hung them around town. We also handed them out to every customer who came into the mercantile. We could do that for yours, too."

Gerda put the skirt she had finished hemming on a shelf and turned around. "But what do we have to do that day?"

Marja smiled. "You're open for business, but it would be nice to have some tea or coffee for your customers. We could even bake cookies to serve people. Something like that would keep people talking about the Dress Emporium."

Anna wanted to do whatever it took to make the store successful. It would be proof that she could take care of herself—that she didn't need a man to make her life complete.

❧

The day of the special opening dawned bright and clear. Anna and Gerda arrived at the shop early to get everything ready.

"I wonder if anyone will even come?" Anna couldn't keep from doubting.

"Well, I'm here." A masculine voice boomed from the doorway of the mercantile. "I heard there were coffee and cookies for hungry men." August's laugh filled the room.

Anna laughed with him. "I'm not sure they're for men. . . unless you want to order a dress or buy some lacy gloves."

Gerda giggled and hugged her brother. Then she poured him a cup of coffee and gave him two large oatmeal raisin cookies.

"Is that all I get?" he teased, as he took a big bite of the spicy treat.

Anna tried to look stern. "We want to have enough for real customers."

August stopped chewing for a moment and took a swig of the beverage.

"I might be a customer. Have you thought of making clothing for men?"

The question shocked Anna, and she could tell from the look on Gerda's face that she was also surprised.

"Why don't you buy your clothing from the mercantile?" Anna blurted.

August's mouth was full of a bite of cookie, so he chewed it up before he answered. "I could, but they don't often have anything that really fits me."

Anna knew why. A big man with a barrel chest and muscled arms, he couldn't wear regular-sized clothing. Then a picture of herself trying to take his measurements dropped into her mind. Heat climbed her neck and cheeks. She was sure that everyone in the room could see them glow.

"That's why I ask *Moder* to make my shirts. I can usually find trousers and overalls that fit. It's the shirts that are a problem." August set his empty cup down. "Mor won't let me pay her, so I thought maybe the two of you could help me. I'm a grown man. I shouldn't be taking advantage of my mother's generosity."

"Could you bring us one of the shirts Mor made you so we can use it for a pattern?" Gerda probably didn't know that she was rescuing Anna from her thoughts.

"I'll bring one the next time I come."

Anna looked toward the stacks of material they had on the shelves behind the counter. "Would you like to pick out the fabric you want us to use? We have several pieces that would work for a man's shirt."

The rest of the opening went well. A steady stream of people came into the shop all day. Some only wanted to look at the new store, but many of them became customers. At the end of the day, Anna and Gerda agreed that the opening had been successful.

❧

Several months went by, and winter melted into spring. The Dress Emporium was thriving so much that Gerda and Anna could barely keep up with the orders. One day Marja entered their workroom, full of excitement. "I have another idea," she said when she was barely into the store.

Gerda and Anna put down the items they were working on and went out into the shop to give her their full attention.

"So tell us." Anna leaned on the empty counter.

Marja wandered around the shop fingering various items as she talked. "I'm tired of living above the store. Even though we expanded the apartment when we bought the building next door, it's still above a store." She picked up a pair of gloves and started trying them on. "The mercantile has been successful for several years. I've convinced Johan that we should build a house to live in." She pulled the gloves off and laid them back on the small round table. Then she turned toward Anna and Gerda. "We won't want the apartment to sit empty. Johan suggested that we offer it to the two of you. Would you like to live here over your shop?"

Anna looked at Gerda. For a moment, they were both speechless. Living over the store would have advantages. They would be close. If they wanted to go home for a few minutes, they could. It wouldn't take them long to get home after work either. Ideas buzzed through Anna's head. It would add to her independence. After all, she was in her midtwenties, not a child anymore.

Gerda looked hopeful. . .then doubtful. "I'm not sure Mor and Far would let me live in town."

Suddenly, Anna doubted whether her parents would agree either. But it was something she had to try. "We won't know until we ask them, will we?"

Marja looked from Gerda to Anna. "The question is, if your parents agree, would you want to live there?"

"Yes," Gerda and Anna said at the same time, and they grabbed each other and hugged.

"It would be wonderful," Anna gushed, sounding more like a child than a businesswoman.

❧

August was tired when he finished shoeing two teams of horses. He would have liked to go back to the boardinghouse and maybe read a book after eating, but Gerda had been insistent that he go to their parents' home for dinner. When he had bathed and put on clean clothes, he did feel better. After mounting his big stallion, he set out in the cold evening air.

Mother had outdone herself with the meal, and August ate more than he usually did. That was saying a lot, because he never pushed back from the table very soon. All through the jovial meal, he wondered why Gerda had insisted that they all come home, but she didn't mention anything special. After everyone was through eating, she asked Gustaf and August to help her clean up the dishes while Olina and Olga entertained their parents. When they finished putting everything away, Gerda urged them into the parlor.

"Okay, Gerda." Bennel Nilsson looked at his daughter.

"What is the big secret? We're all anxious to hear it."

Gerda glanced around the room while Gustaf scooped up his tiny daughter and sat on the velvet sofa beside his wife. "I wanted all of you here, so we could make a good decision."

"About what?" August wanted her to hurry and get it over with so he could return to town.

"Well. . ." Gerda rubbed her hands down the sides of her skirt as if her palms were sweating. It must be something really important to her. "Marja made an offer to Anna and me today. She and Johan are going to build a house to live in." She glanced around the quiet room, as if trying to see if there was a reaction to what she said. "They don't want the apartment above the store to be empty when they move, so she asked if Anna and I would like to live there."

The silence was deafening before pandemonium broke out with everyone speaking.

Bennel held up his hand. "Let's not all talk at once." They all quieted down. "Let's look at this rationally."

"There are some good reasons to do it." Gerda sounded breathless, but eager.

"And there are equally as many reasons not to do it," her father added. "I'm not sure I would be comfortable with you living in town. It could be dangerous."

August had been watching Gerda's hopeful face. When Father said that, her hopes seemed to melt away.

"It might be a good idea." August winked at his sister. "And since I live in town, I could keep an eye on Gerda and Anna." Especially Anna. It would be good to have her so close. He could go by the store or the apartment to check on his sister, and Anna would be there, too. The thought made his heart beat a little faster. Maybe with Anna close by, he could break through the facade she had built around herself and reach the woman he knew was deep inside. Maybe Anna would wear that wedding dress for him. He was tempted to buy it the next time he went to the store.

seven

Anna had a headache. This discussion was making her tired and cranky. All she wanted was for it to be over so she could go to bed. Why had she thought it would be a good idea to wait until after dinner to ask her parents about moving to town when the Braxtons finished building their new house? If she had asked earlier, maybe the decision would be made by now. She rubbed her temples in a circular motion, trying to relieve the stress and pain.

"Anna, Dear, are you all right?" Margreta Jenson leaned toward her daughter.

Anna looked up and nodded. She didn't want them to stop talking before a decision was made. The right decision, that she and Gerda could move into the apartment.

Ollie had always been closer to Anna than Lowell, even though Lowell was only one year older and Ollie one year younger than she was. His sympathetic perusal soothed her.

"I've listened to all the concerns you've brought up, Fader." This was the first addition Ollie made to the conversation. "I agree that we need to be careful of our Anna."

Soren Jenson gave a tight smile and nodded. He seemed to be glad that his son agreed with him.

"But," Ollie continued, "Anna is a grown woman. I feel that she and Gerda would be as safe in town as they are riding alone from the farms to the store each day. Maybe even safer. Besides, one or the other of us usually goes into town at least every other day. Sometimes more often. We could always check on them."

Soren tented his fingers and leaned his chin against them. Sitting with his eyes closed, he often used this position when he was thinking.

"You know that August Nilsson lives in town." Finally, Lowell sounded as if he were on Anna's side in this. "He'll go by to see Gerda when he can, and the Braxtons have treated the girls almost as if they were family. This might be a good thing for Anna. I, for one, am glad to see her so interested in something after all she's been through."

Lowell looked at Anna as if he were sorry to bring it up and cause her further pain. But she knew what he was doing, and she appreciated it.

Soren leaned forward with his forearms on his legs, hands dangling between his knees. "Okay, boys. You've convinced me."

Anna smiled.

"But," he continued as he sat up and looked at her with a stern expression, "at the first sign of trouble, Anna's coming home. That's my final word on it."

❧

The next morning, Anna strode into the Dress Emporium late. After her bout with the headache, she had overslept. At least this morning, she felt good. As she walked into the workroom, she took off her coat, riding hat, and gloves.

Gerda sat in a straight chair by a window as she sewed buttons on a shirt for August. Anna was glad he had picked out that particular plaid. A thin line of bright yellow set off the interwoven blues and grays—hues that complemented his coloring.

Gerda let the shirt drop into her lap as she looked at Anna. "Well, how did it go at your house last night?" When Anna grimaced, Gerda continued, "Was it that bad?"

After placing her gloves in the pocket, Anna hung her coat

and hat on a large hook on the back wall. "It went on a long time. I don't think Far would have agreed if it hadn't been for Lowell and Ollie."

Gerda smiled. "I know what you mean. Our discussion wasn't that long, but I'm thankful that August said he would check on me often. I think that made the difference."

Anna turned and laughed. "Your parents said it was okay, too?"

Gerda put the shirt on a table and came to give Anna a hug. "Yes. Can you believe it? It's really going to happen."

"Have you told Johan and Marja yet?"

"No, I was waiting to see if everything went okay at your house. My parents wouldn't let me live here alone."

When Gerda and Anna went to talk to Marja, they found her at the back counter, poring over several books. She looked up as they approached. "You both look happy. Do you have good news for me?"

After the young women finished explaining that they were going to move into the apartment, Marja told them to come behind the counter with her. She wanted them to see the books of house plans that she was studying. Johan had ordered three from different architectural firms so Marja could pick out the house she wanted.

"How long will it take for the plans to get here?" Anna wanted to know.

"Oh, we already have them." Marja smiled. "We've even ordered the lumber and supplies required by the plans. They are coming on a railcar today. I'm looking at the books again because they're interesting."

Gerda opened the one from Palliser & Palliser Company in Connecticut. Anna picked up the *Specimen Book* from Bicknells & Company in New York.

"Which house plan did you choose?" Anna glanced from the book she held to Marja.

Marja picked up *American Domestic Architecture* from John Calvin Stevens and Albert Winslow Cobb in New York. "I liked the houses in this one best." After she flipped through the pages, she placed the open book on the counter so all three of them could look at it. "I chose this one."

Spread out before them was a house like no other in Litchfield. It had two stories and an attic with a triple window in the gable that faced the front. Windows at ground level indicated a basement, too.

"They have plans for a house with a basement or without. I think we'll do the one without. It won't take as long to build. I'm anxious to have the house finished."

"It's a big house for only two people." The minute the words left her mouth, Anna was sorry for what she said. She put the fingers of her right hand over her mouth as if to catch the words, but it was too late. She knew that although they had wanted children, Johan and Marja had never had any.

"That's all right, Anna." Marja gave her a quick hug. "We have a large family. When they come to visit, we don't have room for many of them. Most of them have to stay at the hotel. With this house, we can invite all of them for Christmas, and they can stay with us. That's what we are planning to do this year."

Anna was grateful for the way Marja thought about everyone else's feelings. It helped her, but she decided to be more careful with her words in the future.

"Actually, I'm through with these books right now." Marja closed them one at a time and stacked them on top of each other. "If you girls would like to take them to look at, you can."

The idea brought a pang to Anna's heart. She hadn't been

able to completely get rid of the desire to have a home and a family to go with it. Looking at house plans would be too much, but Gerda didn't share her aversion.

"Thank you, Marja," she said, as she gathered them into her arms. "We'll return them when we've looked at them all."

"I have an idea." Marja seemed always to be full of new ideas. "Why don't I take you up to the apartment? I don't think you've been there since we enlarged it."

When they arrived at the top of the stairs that went up the outside of the building, Marja pulled a skeleton key from her pocket. After swinging the door open, she gestured for Gerda and Anna to go in before her.

Anna had always loved the look of the parlor. Marja had a good eye for decorating. The furniture contained decorative pillows and doilies, as well as many knickknacks. Pleasing prints of floral paintings adorned the walls, along with family portraits.

Anna and Gerda had been in the dining room and kitchen of the apartment, but never in the bedroom. They were amazed to find that there were two separate bedrooms. When they moved in, they would have plenty of privacy. Anna was even more glad that they would be living there soon.

❧

The large Scandinavian community at Litchfield was a close one. They helped each other whenever needed. Everyone at the church knew Johan and Marja. When Johan announced that they were going to build a house, the men started planning how they could help. Many of the families had built their own homes when they came to Minnesota. And there had been several times when there had been a community-wide barn raising when a neighbor needed a place for his animals.

Johan hired a carpenter to oversee the work, and most of the men in the church planned to give one week to help with the building. This was a major social event, too. The women would cook plenty of food for everyone.

On Monday, August didn't open the blacksmith shop. He had worked especially hard to finish all the projects on Saturday. He planned to help Johan all week, if there were no emergencies that needed his attention. Everyone was going to be there the first day they started the house, but the rest of the men would divide into two work teams that would alternate days. That way they could keep up with what needed to be done at home, too.

When August arrived at the lot where the house was going to be built, only a few others were there. They had much farther to come than those who lived in town.

"August, my friend," Johan hailed from the vacant lot next door, where he stood beside stacks and stacks of lumber and other building supplies. "Welcome." Johan strode over to where August stood. "I'm thankful for your help with our project." He clapped August on the back.

August laughed. "You never know when you can return the favor for me."

"I would like that."

I would, too. August looked forward to building a house for himself and his family, when God saw fit to give him a wife. Although he had helped with other houses and barns, he had never worked on anything as elaborate as what Johan had planned. There was even a stack of red bricks with boards holding them up out of the snow. August had never used house plans drawn by an architect before.

It didn't take long for the area to fill with men carrying tools. The carpenter divided them into teams and assigned them specific tasks. August was glad that he and Gustaf were on the same team. They always worked well together. At least since they were adults, they had. Soon the sound of saws and hammers filled the air, interspersed with conversations that often had to be shouted over the other sounds. The crisp air had a festive feeling, even though they were working hard.

August's stomach had given a rumble loud enough for his teammates to hear when the first wagon containing women pulled into the vacant lot on the opposite side from the materials. The aromas of various foods wafted on the slight breeze, enticing the men's attention.

When August walked over to the first wagon, another conveyance joined it. He was glad to see Gerda and Anna in the second vehicle.

"Do you ladies need help setting up?" He couldn't take his eyes off Anna.

Her cheeks were kissed into a becoming pink by the cool air, and strands of hair had worked their way out of her severe bun. He liked to see the thin cloud of dark hair that surrounded her face, giving it a soft frame.

Gerda stretched her leg over the wagon wheel and dropped to the ground. August immediately moved to the other side where Anna was gathering together a couple of bags that were at her feet. He reached up and placed his large hands on her waist. When he lifted her down, it felt as if she weighed no more than a feather.

❧

Anna had been aware of August from the first moment she had seen him while they were driving up. She tried to ignore the feelings that stirred inside her. When his hands touched her waist, the connection was powerful. She was thankful that he let go of her as soon as her feet reached the ground. She looked up to thank him and found him standing much too close for comfort. She took a step backwards and moved around him so she could start unloading the food.

"Let me set up some tables first." August marched across to the supplies and found a couple of sawhorses that weren't being used. He brought them back, set them a few feet apart, and started laying lumber on them.

Gustaf came up carrying two more sawhorses. "That table won't be large enough, if I know our women. Let's use these, too."

Anna watched the brothers as they worked together. She was glad that they were her friends. They were two godly men who lived their faith. It was too bad that she and Gustaf weren't meant to be together. Actually, she wasn't meant to be married to any man. Or so it seemed. She couldn't understand why God had created her with this flaw, whatever it was, that kept a man from loving her enough. Maybe He wanted her to love Him more. . .and be an independent businesswoman. Anna shook her head and went to join the other women as they spread sheets on the wood and started placing heaping bowls and platters of hot food on the makeshift tables.

Marja came to where Gerda and Anna worked. "I wanted to talk to the two of you."

Anna turned toward her, but Gerda continued arranging food while she listened.

"I have ordered some furniture for the parlor in the new house. If you would like, I can leave the parlor furniture in the apartment for you to use. Then all you would need to find would be bedroom furniture for each of you."

Margreta Jenson walked up while Marja was speaking. "Anna, you may take the furniture from your bedroom at the house. Your father and I talked about it last night. We wanted to help you that way. And we probably have some tables and lamps in the attic that you can use."

Gerda stopped what she was doing and turned toward them. "Mor and Far told me last night that I can have the furniture from my bedroom, too. They still have quite a few things that Mrs. Johnson left when she sold the farm to them. It's all stored in our attic. Mor said that we can take our pick of anything we need. Oh, Anna, God is working everything out so well."

❧

By the end of the first week, all of the internal and external walls of the house were completed. August planned to give some time each day to help with the finishing. It was a good thing that Johan had hired a woodworker to do the banisters and kitchen cabinets. He had even brought a bricklayer from Minneapolis. August was going to learn as much as he could from each of these men. While he worked on the house, he began to envision a house he would someday build. Maybe he would borrow one of those books from Johan. Those detailed plans made a big difference in how fast they could build. With all the help, the Braxtons could probably move in two or three weeks. A month at the most.

When he finished working on Saturday, he stopped by the Dress Emporium to talk to Gerda. Anna was busy with a customer, but Gerda was in the workroom, ironing a dress. He stood in the doorway, watching Anna as she talked to a young woman and her brother. The brother had helped with building the house this week. They were fairly new to town, but he had been a hard worker.

"August, did you come to see me?" Gerda was finished with the dress.

"Yes." August watched her place the flatiron back on the stove. "I was wondering how soon after the Braxtons move to their house that you and Anna will want to move into the apartment."

Gerda glanced toward the showroom. "We've been talking about that. Both of us want to move as soon as we can. Tomorrow afternoon Anna is going to come to our house so we can look at the furniture that is stored in the attic. We'll pick out what we want to use."

"That sounds like a good idea. I suppose you want all your brothers to help you get your furniture to the apartment."

Gerda placed her hands against her waist and tried to frown at him. "Of course we do. What are brothers for?"

After they shared a laugh, August started back through the store. He glanced toward Anna and the people she was waiting on. He couldn't help noticing how the man was trying to flirt with Anna. A sword pierced his heart. A remnant of the jealousy he thought he had conquered spilled inside him, spreading its venom. He clenched his fists and strode out the front door to keep from saying or doing anything that would upset Anna. When he reached the sidewalk, he turned and glanced through the window. Anna was laughing with the man about something. The sword thrust deeper inside him.

eight

August spent every free hour he had working on the house with Johan and the others. As he pounded nails or wielded a paint brush, he was fighting to get the jealousy under control again. He only went back to the Dress Emporium one time after seeing the farmer flirt with Anna. Anytime August saw Anna, the picture of her laughing up at the man flew into his mind. When he was back at the boardinghouse in the evening, that thought led to others. Memories of all the times Gustaf had been with Anna, when August wished he was the one with her.

The more August tried to fight the feelings of jealousy, the harder the thoughts assaulted his mind. He knew what the apostle Paul was talking about when he taught about the fiery darts of Satan. August felt sure that these memories were part of Satan's attack on him. He longed for the time when he had been able to control his thoughts.

So as he worked, he tried to stay away from as many of the other men as he could. He was afraid to participate in the conversations. Afraid some of this poison would spill out and be revealed to others. And he didn't want anyone else to know his shame.

"August," Gustaf called to him when it was about quitting time. "How would you like to come over for dinner tonight? I think Gerda and Anna will be there to cook so Olina will have a rest."

August finally turned toward his brother, but he kept his

gaze on the ground. "Actually, I am so tired that all I want is a hot bath and to go to bed." When he looked up at Gustaf's face, he could tell that Gustaf didn't think he meant what he said, but he turned back to do the last few strokes of painting he was working on.

The workers would be finished with the Braxtons' house that week. Marja and Johan would move in next week, then Gerda and Anna would be ready to take possession of the apartment.

❧

Anna woke early and dressed in old clothes. Moving day had finally arrived. After eating the breakfast her mother prepared while Anna was dressing, she hurried back upstairs to pack the rest of her things. While she latched her last carpetbag, she heard the wagon pull around to the front of the house. Ollie and Lowell were such good brothers. They insisted that they could get all of her bedroom furniture on the wagon. If they couldn't fit the other things on there with it, Ollie told her he would hitch up the buggy, and she could take the extra items in that.

Anna was halfway down the stairs carrying two bags when Ollie came through the door. Lowell was right behind him.

"Good morning, Sleepyhead." Ollie reached to take the bags from her hands.

"You are such a tease." Anna held tight to the handles. "I can get these. You two can start with the big pieces."

In less than an hour, everything was loaded, and they were headed to town. Anna would probably be there before Lowell and Ollie. Their wagon was piled high with heavy items. All she had in the buggy were her carpetbags and a trunk.

When they got out on the road, Anna pulled around the wagon. "I'll see you in town, slow pokes." Anna waved at her brothers as she passed.

She was not surprised to see that Gerda, August, and Gustaf were already at the apartment. They had two loads of furniture to bring from the Nilsson farm. Anna felt that God was smiling on her the way He provided all their needs for furnishings. Neither she nor Gerda would have to buy anything right away. Of course, they might want to add some decorating touches of their own to all the donated items.

August was coming out the door of the apartment when Anna started up the stairs. She smiled up at him, but he brushed past her as if he was in a real hurry. What was wrong with him? Maybe he was grouchy because he had to get up so early this morning.

"Anna." Gerda stood in the doorway and called to her. "Come see how wonderful everything looks." She swept her arm toward the opening to usher Anna inside.

Anna took a deep breath. Home. This was her home. Hers and Gerda's.

❧

About the time everything had been unloaded and placed where the young women wanted them, Margreta Jenson and Ingrid Nilsson arrived with baskets of food. They bustled around the kitchen setting the table for their six hungry children and themselves.

"Moder." Anna grabbed her and hugged her. "And Mrs. Nilsson, how thoughtful you are. This food smells heavenly."

"I couldn't agree with you more." Gustaf followed his nose to the kitchen.

Soon they were all seated at the large dining room table.

"Gerda," Anna looked around the room, "I thought the table was too large for the two of us when you showed it to me in the attic. But there's plenty of room for it and all the chairs. You've even brought the china cabinet. It's elegant, and we have room for company."

While they shared conversation as well as food, Anna noticed once again that August seemed more quiet than usual. Perhaps something was wrong with him. She hoped that he wasn't sick or something. He had been working hard to help the Braxtons finish building their house. Maybe he was exhausted. She wondered if any of his family had noticed the change in him.

❧

August hoped no one noticed that he was trying to keep out of Anna's way. He tried to act natural. Maybe it was working.

When they finished eating, he returned to the smithy and stirred up the coals in the forge. It didn't take long to get the answer to his unasked question.

About an hour and a half after he left, Gustaf walked through the open door. The sun reflecting off the remnants of the last snowfall cast his shadow across the room. August turned from what he was doing.

"Are you going to tell me what's bothering you?" Gustaf came right to the point.

August looked at the determination on Gustaf's face and decided not to try to lie to him.

"What makes you think something is bothering me?"

"I know you well enough to know when something is bothering you. You were pretty sullen the last week or two that we were building the house. Gerda tells me that you haven't been to the store to check on her for quite awhile, and didn't you promise Far that you would?"

August looked down and scuffed the dirt floor with the toe of his boot. "She hadn't moved to town yet."

"But you used to go see her several times a week." Gustaf sounded stern now. "And I saw how you've been avoiding

Anna. Has something happened to cause you to be rude to her?"

August snorted. He wasn't going to get out of this discussion. He wished that he could disappear into the ground. He didn't want to bare his soul to Gustaf, especially since he had been jealous of him so long. He looked toward the ceiling. *Gud, now would be a good time to intervene.* When nothing happened, he looked at his brother, noticing for the first time that his eyes were filled with compassion. Gustaf really cared.

August turned back to the forge and closed the damper. This could take a long time, and he didn't need a roaring fire getting out of control.

"I'm not sure I know how to tell you what's wrong."

"August, I'm your brother. I love you, and anything you tell me will remain between the two of us." Gustaf leaned against the table that ran along the wall of the smithy. It was his favorite place when he came in to talk to August.

August joined him there. At least it would be easier to explain if they weren't face to face. "I'm fighting some fierce spiritual battles."

After a long pause, Gustaf said, "I know that you don't drink, or gamble, or chase women. So tell me what the battle is about."

"Jealousy." The word hung in the air between them for a long time.

When August didn't say anything else, Gustaf finally asked, "What kind of jealousy?"

August stood up and stalked across the smithy. He stood with his back to his brother, watching the flames grow smaller and smaller as he recited the ugly truth in a monotone.

"I've been jealous of you as long as I can remember. You were the perfect son. And I wasn't." August didn't want to see the expression on Gustaf's face at this pronouncement. "When we came to America, I fell for Anna the first time I saw her. But I was the quiet son. The shy one. Before I could work up my courage to speak to her, there you were charming her. The jealousy increased every time I saw you together."

Finally August couldn't stand it any longer. He turned around to look at Gustaf. His head was bowed, and he looked as if he had been hit in the stomach with a poleax. August hated to rock the boat or upset anyone. This had been harder than he thought it would be. He knew as he looked at the way Gustaf's shoulders drooped that he loved his brother, even though he was jealous of him.

Gustaf raised his head. "When I told Anna that I couldn't see her anymore, why didn't you approach her after that?"

August didn't want to speak this out loud, but he had come this far. He might as well reveal all the ugliness. "I didn't want your castoff."

Gustaf's stricken eyes met his. "How could we have gone so wrong?"

Once more August was disgusted. Disgusted at himself for his weakness. "We haven't gone wrong. I have."

Gustaf came toward August and put his arm over his shoulders. "I think we need to go down to the church. If we sit and talk there, maybe God will give us some special insight."

August nodded. He followed Gustaf out into the cold, sunny day. After closing the big double doors, he dropped a board across them. Gustaf waited for him, and they walked the mile to the church in silence.

Once inside the cool building, the brothers sat on the front pew looking at the cross hung on the wall behind the pulpit. Silence stretched between them, but it wasn't uncomfortable. Each man listened for the voice of God to speak into his heart.

Gustaf got up and stepped onto the platform. On a shelf behind the pulpit, he found the extra Bible the pastor kept there. Picking it up, he returned to sit beside his brother. After turning through several books, he stopped and started reading.

"Here's a verse for you." Gustaf looked up at August before he continued reading. " 'Set me as a seal upon thine heart, as a seal upon thine arm: for love is strong as death; jealousy is cruel as the grave: the coals thereof are coals of fire, which hath a most vehement flame.' I found this in the Song of Solomon the other night."

August looked at him. "I can honestly say that's not a book that I've ever read."

"It says that love is strong as death and jealousy as cruel as the grave. You work with hot coals. You know what they can do when they are allowed to burn hotter and brighter."

August nodded. In the past, he had often studied God's word. Many times he had been refreshed with a new revelation when he read a familiar passage. But he hadn't spent much time in Bible study lately.

"God said that jealousy can burn like a blazing fire. Jealousy can consume you and destroy you the way fire destroys. Jealousy can burn up all that is good inside you."

August thought about that for a minute. "I know that's true. It has been like a fire in my belly, devouring the goodness in me."

"Not all the goodness." Gustaf turned several more pages in the Bible. "Proverbs 27:4 says, 'Wrath is cruel, and anger is outrageous; but who is able to stand before envy?' Envy here is just another word for jealousy."

"I haven't been standing very strong before it." August put his elbows on his knees and dropped his head into his hands. "I've tried, and things get better. Sometimes, the good times last a long time. Then once again I will be overcome with the jealousy."

Gustaf started murmuring words that were too soft for August to hear, but he knew that his brother was praying. When Gustaf finished, he sat as if he were listening again. After a few moments, he once again turned some of the pages.

" 'All the paths of the LORD are mercy and truth unto such as keep his covenant and his testimonies.' That's what Psalm 25:10 says. August, you need to get rid of that jealousy."

August raised his head. "Don't you think I would if I knew how?"

Gustaf patted him on the shoulder. "Maybe part of the problem is that you have been trying to fight it alone. God wants us to share our burdens with those who love us. Besides, there's nothing for you to be jealous of from me. I love you, and I always have. You know that Anna wasn't the person God intended for me to marry. I'm sorry I monopolized her and stood in your way. Can you forgive me?"

August was amazed. Gustaf hadn't done anything wrong. He was an honorable man, both with Anna and with his brothers, and he was apologizing. August looked deep into his own heart. How could he not forgive his brother? "I want to, and I'll try."

"That's all I ask. And I don't want jealousy to destroy the man God intends you to be."

❧

When August got back to the boardinghouse that evening, he did something that he hadn't done for quite awhile. He read his Bible. He reread the verses that Gustaf shared with him, but he read other passages, too. When he finished, he bowed his head and prayed. For the first time in a long time, he wasn't burdened down with the jealousy.

The next morning, he went by the apartment to see if Gerda and Anna would accompany him to church. When he first saw Anna, his heart nearly flipped over. She was so beautiful.

"Of course we'll go to church with you." Gerda took his arm. "We were dreading walking all that way by ourselves."

August hit his forehead with his palm. "Why didn't I think to bring a buggy?"

"It's okay," Anna said as she picked up her reticule. "I don't mind the walk. We sit too much when we work."

During the service, August had a hard time keeping his mind on the sermon. Anna was sitting on the other side of Gerda. He was aware of every tiny move she made. She rearranged her skirt several times. Once she hid a cough behind a handkerchief she pulled from her handbag. He had been so intent on Anna that the service was over before he realized it,.

August took Gerda's arm when she started to get up. "Would you two beautiful ladies let me take you to lunch at the hotel? We could celebrate your move."

During the meal, August tried not to be too obvious about watching Anna. She was the epitome of a gracious, independent woman. But he wished for so much more. At least she hadn't mentioned the new farmer he had seen at the Dress Emporium. There had been no need for August to be jealous of him. It was another lie of Satan that tormented him far too long.

August planned to take a nap after the large meal, but when he returned to his room, he sat in the chair and stared out the window. The feelings he had for Anna were the kind a man should have for the woman he planned to marry. What could he do about that?

He prayed and asked the Lord if Anna was the woman he should marry. The peace that filled his heart seemed to be God's blessing on the match. But August knew that Anna wasn't ready for marriage yet. She was too intent on her new life.

"How can I help her love me?" August knew there was no one there to answer him, so he got up and paced across the room and back. "I'll just have to pray for her and find ways to show her my love." So he started making plans.

nine

Anna turned the skirt she was working on so she could sew the other side seam. When she did, she twisted her hips a little to make them more comfortable. She had been sitting at the sewing machine in one position too long.

"Have you noticed how often August has been coming by the shop?" Anna didn't take her gaze from her work when Gerda spoke to her. The young women often talked while working and were not distracted from their respective tasks.

"He did promise your father that he would check on us often. That's the main reason you were allowed to move into the apartment with me."

Anna came to the end of the seam and stopped pedaling. She cut the thread and tied the two pieces in a knot close to the fabric to keep the seam from pulling apart. She pivoted on her seat, enjoying the cushioning.

Gerda glanced up from the lace insertion she was sewing into a sleeve. "But did he promise to make us a padded sewing chair, too?"

"No. August was being kind." Anna turned back to the sewing machine and started on another seam.

"Yes, he was." Gerda shook the sleeve out before starting to baste it to the rest of the blouse. "Your brothers Lowell and Ollie promised to check on us, too, but they don't come every day. . .and they don't bring us gifts all the time either."

"August doesn't bring gifts all the time."

"The new display tables he made. . .a book of poetry for

the apartment. . .flowers for the showroom. . .a box of Irish linen handkerchiefs with embroidered flowers and dainty lace edging. Actually, he only brought the handkerchiefs to you. Remember, I wasn't here, and he knew I would be spending the day with Olina. Those were only for you."

Anna stood up and held the skirt by the waist so she could shake out any wrinkles. She could feel the heat warming her face. Probably another one of her blushes. Why did she do that? People with fair skin were supposed to be the ones to blush, not her.

"I tried to tell him that he shouldn't give them to me, but he was insistent. . .and they were so pretty. . ."

Gerda laughed.

Anna started folding the skirt. "Well, the padded chair he brought to use with the sewing machine was for both of us."

"August knew that you use the machine much more than I do. I think he made it with you in mind."

Anna laid the folded skirt on the shelf to wait for Gerda to sew the hem by hand. It was time for her to take a break, and she needed to get away from this conversation. She walked into the showroom.

No one had come into the shop all day. She wondered if the Braxtons' store had been busy. Sometimes Wednesdays were slow days for both the mercantile and the Dress Emporium. She decided to go ask Marja about their customers, so she hurried toward the door to the mercantile. She glanced down for a moment and barreled into a rock-hard wall. A warm wall covered with plaid. Plaid with arms that gathered her against it.

At the sound of a deep chuckle, Anna looked up into the eyes of the person she had been talking about for the last half hour. Did their words cause him to arrive? She felt breathless and comfortable all at the same time.

❧

August couldn't believe his good fortune when Anna practically ran into his arms. He knew she was in a hurry to get somewhere and hadn't noticed him. But the feeling of her against his chest was wonderful. He wanted her to stay there forever. *Please, Lord.*

Anna looked up at him. After stepping back, she murmured, "Sorry," and the color in her cheeks intensified.

"That's all right." August chuckled. "I enjoyed it."

Anna hurried around him and headed toward Marja Braxton. What was she running from—him or her own emotions? He hoped it was her emotions. Maybe his prayers and showering her with love were making a difference.

He entered the Dress Emporium. When Gerda wasn't in the showroom, he continued on to the workroom.

"How's my favorite sister?"

Gerda was ironing something soft and white. "I'm your only sister." She placed the flatiron in its holder on the stove and turned around. "What brings you to the shop today? Not more presents?"

August shook his head slightly and looked out the window. He hoped his sister didn't notice how embarrassed he was. He hadn't wanted her to realize what he was doing. Anna was supposed to be the one to notice. "Gustaf came by the smithy this morning. Mor is having one of the hired hands bring dinner to their house tonight so Olina won't have to cook. She said that she'd fix enough for me, too." He moved closer to the window so he could look the other way down the street.

"Anna isn't here right now."

"What?"

"Anna isn't here right now."

When August turned to look at her, she was grinning at him. "Why did you say that?"

"That's why you come so often, isn't it? To see Anna."

His sister was much too perceptive, but he wasn't going to tell her that.

❧

Gustaf had told August to come right in when he arrived, so August opened the door and walked in. Taking a deep whiff of the tantalizing aroma of his mother's cooking, he followed his nose to the kitchen. Gustaf had Olga in the high chair that August had built for her. She was banging a spoon on the table while her father set the plates around the edge.

"Do you need some help?" August lifted Olga from her perch.

"Unka!" she screamed before throwing her arms around his neck and squeezing. "High."

August swung her up and down while Gustaf finished getting the food on the table. "You're pretty good at that."

Gustaf looked up from what he was doing. "Kitchen work is awkward for me, but it's one way I can help Olina." He folded his arms across his chest. "She's miserable today."

"Is she coming down for supper?"

"I don't know. I'll go ask."

While Gustaf was upstairs, August started feeding his hungry niece.

After the meal was over, Gustaf started back up the stairs. Olina hadn't wanted to eat when everyone else did. She told him to see if she was hungry when they finished.

August took Olga to the parlor.

"Horsey, Unka."

He had been heading for the rocking chair, but he chose

the settee instead. He sat down and crossed his legs. After lowering Olga to sit on his top foot, he kept a tight hold on her hands and started moving his foot up and down.

"Ride a little horsey, up and down."

The trouble with starting this game was that Olga never wanted to quit. It was one of her favorite things to do. After what seemed like a thousand times of kicking his leg up and down giving Olga a ride on his foot, August was glad that his brother finally returned. Gustaf rubbed his hand over his eyes as he came into the room.

"Does Olina want her supper now?" August pulled Olga up into his lap. His leg was tired, so he was glad for this reprieve.

"No." Gustaf reached down and took his daughter. He hugged her tight. "She has gone into labor. I feel so helpless, watching her hurt."

August stood. "I'll take Olga to town. I'm sure Anna would be glad to spend time with her. I can bring Gerda back. Then I'll go to the farm to get *Moder.*"

❧

Anna had taken her hair down to prepare it for bed. She brushed it out before making a long braid. She liked to have it out of her way when she changed from her everyday clothes to her nightdress. When she finished brushing, a loud knock sounded on the door to the apartment. Who could that be? Maybe Gerda would see.

"Anna," Gerda called through the wall. "Can you answer the door? I'm not dressed."

The knock sounded again, more insistent this time. It must be important. Anna pushed her hair behind her back and hurried across the parlor.

"Who is it?" she called through the door.

"August."

What could he want at this time of night? Then Anna heard a tiny voice. She pulled the door wide to allow August to enter with his burden. The night was cool, so Olga was bundled into a quilt. Anna took her and started unwrapping the large cover.

"Why are you and Olga on our doorstep?" Anna glanced to where August had stood, but he had disappeared out the door.

Olga began whimpering again. Anna pulled her close and hummed as she patted her back. This little girl should be asleep by now.

Gerda came into the parlor. "What are you doing with Olga?"

"I don't know." Anna dropped a kiss on the little girl's droopy head.

Gerda went to the door. When she opened it, August arrived at the top of the stairs with his arms full.

"Olina is going to have the baby soon. I brought Olga to you, Anna." He placed a large cloth bag on the settee. "Here are all the things she'll need tonight. Do you mind taking care of her?"

Anna looked at August's concerned expression. "Of course not. I love Olga."

"Are you going to take me to Olina?" Gerda was already heading toward her bedroom. "That's wonderful." She turned back and hugged her brother before she left the room. "I'll throw together a few things in case I have to stay with her awhile."

When August and Gerda left, Anna sat in the rocking chair until Olga slept soundly. She laid Olga on the carpet in her bedroom while she pushed her bed against the wall. Then she put the little angel on the bed close to the wall.

After changing her own clothes, she climbed in beside her and started praying for Olina.

❧

Anna decided not to open the shop the next morning. She wanted to wait until she heard from Gerda. After she and Olga had breakfast together, she spent the morning playing with the little girl. Every time she picked Olga up, her heart longed for a child of her own.

Anna knew that her whole being reacted whenever August was around, and it had seemed that he might be interested in her, but she couldn't trust those feelings. Her relationship with Gustaf had seemed strong, but it wasn't enough for him to love her. Then, when she was going to marry Olaf, she loved him, but he didn't love her enough to heed her warnings. No, feelings weren't enough to overcome whatever it was that was wrong with her that kept a man from loving her enough.

After lunch, Anna rocked Olga so she would take a nap. When she was asleep, instead of putting her down on the pallet, Anna held her and imagined that she was holding her own child. Tears streamed down her cheeks as she grieved for what she would never have.

Anna heard the key turn in the door before Gerda quietly stepped into the room. Anna was thankful that Gerda probably knew Olga would be napping. She turned her face away, trying to hide the tears. With one hand, she wiped her cheeks before she greeted Gerda.

"Has Olina had the baby?"

Gerda sank onto the settee. "No. She's having a long, hard labor. Mor told me to come help you with Olga."

She reached to take her niece from Anna's arms. After hugging her softly, she laid her on the pallet in Anna's bedroom. When she returned to the parlor, Anna had finished drying her cheeks. She hoped there weren't too many other traces of crying on her face.

"Do you want me to stay with Olga, or should I go open the shop?" Gerda hid a yawn behind her hand.

"Did you get any sleep last night?"

Gerda shook her head.

"Why don't you take a nap while Olga does? She should be tired enough to sleep a long time. We played all morning." Anna started for the door. "I'll go to the shop."

❧

The sun was starting to go down when August rode into town. All day he had a hard time thinking about anything but Anna with her beautiful hair hanging down her back. When he had seen her, for a moment it chased all other thoughts from his head. He wanted to touch the waves that tumbled like a waterfall down her back. He was sure the strands would feel soft as silk. He had had to leave abruptly to retrieve Olga's things. It allowed him time to take control of his longings.

Anna was locking the door to the shop when he stopped in front of the store. She quickly turned. "Have you heard anything yet?"

He dismounted and came to stand by her. She stepped farther into the waning sunlight.

"Olina and Gustaf have a son." A smile split his face.

"How is Olina?"

"Mother and son are doing fine. Do you want me to take Olga now?"

Anna shook her head. "Why don't we keep her here another night? That will give everyone time to get a little rest." She quickly turned and headed toward the stairs at the side of the building.

August wished he had some reason to accompany Anna to

the apartment. But he felt as if she had dismissed him from her presence. Would he ever understand that woman?

When August went to the post office to pick up his mail, the postmaster asked if he wanted to take Gustaf's to him. Olina had received a fat packet from Sweden. August thanked the man and headed to the boardinghouse. The mail could wait until morning.

After August had eaten, he fell into bed. Even though he was exhausted, sleep eluded him. *Lord, what am I going to do about Anna?*

August didn't expect an answer, but a quiet voice spoke into his mind.

Love her.

How was he supposed to do that? He thought that was what he had been doing.

Pray for her.

Somehow, lying on his back didn't seem the right way to pray. So August got up and opened his Bible on the edge of the bed. Then he dropped to his knees on the floor beside the open book. He prayed for Anna's heart to heal and for her relationship with the heavenly Father to increase. And he prayed that somehow Anna would come to love him as much as he loved her.

❧

It was early afternoon before August could pick up Olga to take her home. This time, he rode his stallion. Olga always enjoyed being cradled in August's lap while he was on the big horse. They had often ridden this way, with her snuggled close against his chest.

When they arrived, Gustaf was already waiting at the hitching post. August knew that he had missed his young daughter, and Olga lunged into her father's arms with a squeal. August hoped that someday he would have a daughter who loved him as much.

He followed Gustaf into the house, carrying Olga's bag and the mail, which had been in his saddlebags. "The postmaster gave me your mail. Olina received something from Sweden."

Gustaf put Olga down, and she ran into her grandmother's arms. "Olina will want to see this. Why don't I take it up first? We'll bring Olga to see her *moder* and baby brother later."

He bounded up the stairs. August stayed in the kitchen with their mother. Soon Gustaf returned.

"The letter is from Olina's mother. Her great aunt Olga passed away, and she left Olina quite a bit of money." Gustaf went to the stove and poured a cup of coffee. After taking a sip, he continued. "I've been saving to build onto the house, now that we have two children and are planning to have more. Olina wants me to start as soon as possible." He turned a chair backwards and straddled it with his crossed arms leaning on the back. "I don't suppose you'd be able to help me any time soon, would you?"

Since Gustaf has already drawn plans for the rooms he wanted, August agreed to help him. Even working only part of each day, they should be able to complete it in less than a month.

It took two weeks for all the building materials Gustaf ordered to arrive. When August finished work that afternoon, he rented a wagon from the livery and drove a load to Gustaf. It took them two more trips with both that wagon and Gustaf's to retrieve all of it. August promised to take the next day off to help get the framing up.

Gustaf clapped August on the shoulder. "Why don't you come for breakfast? Mor is still here, and I know she'll be glad to make enough for both her sons."

"I've never been known to turn down my mother's cooking."

They had finished enjoying thick slabs of ham, red-eye gravy, mounds of scrambled eggs, and piping hot biscuits dripping with butter when several men on horses rode up to the house. Gustaf excused himself from the table and went to see who it was. August started to help his mother clear the table.

"You go on now. I'll take care of this." Ingrid Nilsson had to stand on tiptoe to kiss her son's cheek.

August went out to join Gustaf. About a dozen men from their church were milling around the front yard. August wondered how they found out that Gustaf needed help. He was sure Gustaf hadn't told anyone else. But secrets were hard to keep in this close-knit community. Everyone cared about his neighbors. Probably Johan told them that the supplies had arrived. With all this help, they would finish the addition quickly.

Gustaf divided up the work among the men, according to their areas of expertise. When everyone started work, Gustaf and August worked side by side.

August tried to keep his mind on the rooms they were building, but he had a hard time not thinking about Anna. Sometimes, he even whispered a prayer for her when she made her way into his thoughts.

At noon, several women arrived, bringing food for the whole crew. August had enjoyed all the talk the men engaged in when they worked, but after he filled his plate, he sat down under a tree away from the crowd. Soon Gustaf joined him.

"You've been distracted today, haven't you?" Gustaf picked up a piece of fried chicken and bit into it.

August finished chewing before he replied. "Yes. At least it didn't interfere with my work."

"Is it Anna?"

August nodded. "I've been praying for her every day. And I try to go by there as often as I can. I'm not sure how to get through to her."

Gustaf laughed. "I hear you've been taking presents to the girls—especially Anna."

"Did she say something about that?"

"No." Gustaf picked up half a roll dripping with butter, popped it into his mouth, and chewed it up. "Gerda has noticed that everything you do directly affects Anna."

August looked up from his plate. "Do you think Anna knows?"

"I'm not sure. I think you would be good for Anna, and I want to see her happy. I'm going to start praying more earnestly for the two of you. That God would show you His will for your lives."

ten

In early May, Anna changed the navy wool suit that was in the window of the shop. Many women had asked about the new fashions for spring and summer. Anna and Gerda kept up with the new clothing, hats, and accessories offered in the catalogues and fashion magazines they received. Anna had made herself a new spring outfit, but she was going to leave it in the window for awhile before she wore it. Made of soft cream-colored lawn, it was sprigged with tiny blue flowers. The clean lines looked good on Anna's tall frame, but the style could be adapted to many figure types. When she returned the dress form to the window, she glanced at the traffic outside. As the weather warmed, the streets were often filled with people moving about—on foot, on horseback, or in a variety of conveyances.

Her gaze drifted to a buggy she had never seen before. The brass fittings were shined until they sparkled. Even though it came from the direction of the road out of town, the vehicle was so clean, it looked as if it had recently been washed.

The man driving it was dressed in a suit that would have looked good on a banker back East. With his cravat arranged in that manner, Anna thought she could see the sparkle of a diamond nestled in the folds. Surely he wasn't wearing a diamond stickpin in Litchfield, Minnesota. Anna had never seen one before, but she had read about them in the fashion magazines she and Gerda subscribed to.

Sitting beside the man was an exquisitely beautiful young

woman. She looked much too young to be his wife. Maybe she was his daughter. Anna couldn't help wondering what had brought them to this Midwestern town.

"Did you see that couple?" Anna hadn't realized that Gerda stood behind her until she spoke.

"Yes. I wonder who they are."

Anna didn't have to wonder long, because later that afternoon, the newcomers entered the mercantile. After browsing through the merchandise for half an hour, they came into the Dress Emporium. Anna was rearranging several of the displays on the small tables that were scattered around the room and on the sideboard by the wall.

"Oh. . .Father. Look at this wonderful shop." The young woman released her hold on the man's arm and picked up a triangular lacy shawl. She pulled it around her and tried to look over her shoulders to see the back.

"We have a large mirror." Anna pointed toward the cheval glass.

When the young woman walked over, Anna tipped the top of the frame forward a little so the girl could get a better look. She preened before the mirror. The soft blue shawl set off the color of her eyes. When she shook her head, black ringlets tumbled down her back. Anna had seen pictures of china dolls that looked like this girl.

"I like it." The young woman smiled at the man who had been standing to the side watching her every move. "May I have it. . .Father?"

He came to stand behind her and looked over her shoulder at her reflection in the mirror. "How could I deny my precious daughter anything her heart desires?"

The question sounded innocent enough, but Anna wondered at the undercurrent she sensed pulsing between the two.

Then she was distracted when the man walked toward her.

"May I introduce myself?" His smiling eyes sought out Anna's. He extended his hand toward her. "My name is Pierre Le Blanc, and this is my daughter, Rissa."

When Anna reached to shake his hand, he instead grasped the tips of her fingers and lifted them to his mouth. When his lips touched her, shivers went up her spine. She had never had a man kiss her hand before, but she had read about it in books. His moist lips moved ever so slightly against her fingers, causing his moustache to tickle her.

Anna didn't know what to think about this. It wasn't unpleasant, but the awkwardness she felt made her stand aloof. She hoped that he would recognize that she didn't welcome his advances. Unfortunately, that aloofness seemed to draw the man more than if she had fawned over him. When Anna moved toward the counter, Mr. Le Blanc followed her. She stepped behind the wooden structure, hoping to put space between them, but the man leaned casually on the counter, as if he were trying to get closer to her.

❧

August had taken a horse back to the livery stable when the fancy buggy pulled in the door. The dandy who was driving it looked down his nose at the big blacksmith. August didn't like to feel like some sort of insect being flicked away by the man. *Who does he think he is?*

"Here's the horse I shod." August addressed Hank, the owner of the livery, and ignored the newcomer. "Do any of the other horses need shoeing?"

When Hank shook his head, August returned to the blacksmith shop. He hurried to finish his work because he wanted to go to the Dress Emporium and see if Gerda or Anna knew who that man was. For some inexplicable reason,

August had the feeling that the man was up to no good.

When August finally arrived at the shop, Anna was nowhere around, but he found Gerda in the workroom. "Did you see the new man who came into town this morning?" August didn't mean for his question to sound harsh, but it did.

Gerda looked up from her work. "Hello, Brother, I'm glad to see you, too." She put the garment she was hemming on the table and went to hug him. He was sure she was glad that he took time to clean up before he came to see her. "Now what is this about the new visitors in town?"

"Did they come here?"

Gerda nodded, but looked away from her brother's scrutiny.

"So what are you not telling me?" August leaned his shoulder against the doorframe and crossed his ankles. He hoped he looked relaxed, but he didn't feel it.

"Mr. Le Blanc and his daughter came into the shop earlier." Gerda turned toward August.

"He has a daughter?"

"Yes, her name is Rissa. Kind of a strange name, isn't it? And she's very beautiful—in a china doll kind of way."

August digested that piece of information. "How old is his daughter?"

"I don't know. She was very dainty. At first, I thought she was only a girl, but after she was here awhile, I realized that she was probably a young woman. Why are you so interested in them?"

August stood up away from the door facing and walked over to look out the window, with his arms crossed over his chest. "I didn't see the girl. Only the man. . .and he wasn't very friendly."

Gerda laughed. "He wasn't very friendly to me either, but he was to Anna."

August felt a slow burn start in his stomach and move upward inside him. A return of the old jealousy? "Just how friendly was he?"

Gerda liked to tease her brothers, and she took the chance to do it now. "Well. . .he did kiss her hand."

August whirled around to face her. "Kiss her hand?" burst from his lips. "Why did he kiss her hand?"

Anna walked in the room in time to hear the outburst. "It was only a friendly gesture."

August glared at her. "Friendly gesture? Well, here's a friendly gesture for you." He stomped toward Anna, took her by her shoulders, and pressed his lips to hers.

It was a brief kiss, but suddenly everything changed for August. He hurried out the door as if he were being chased. Why in the world did he do that? Anna looked shocked, and he felt as if his heart had been ripped out. He wanted the first time he kissed Anna to be special. Tender, soft, and a prelude to a long life together, not a jealous gesture in anger. Now he had ruined everything. His inability to control jealousy had caused Anna pain.

❧

While August ran away, Anna stood touching her lips with the fingertips of her right hand. Why had August done that? She had begun to feel drawn to him, and here he had kissed her in anger. What had she done to make him angry? When she looked at Gerda, she had returned to hemming the dress, and a smile covered her face. What was there to smile about?

Before Anna could ask her, the bell over the door of the shop jingled. Anna went to see who had entered and found Mr. Le Blanc and Rissa.

"My daughter would like to order some dresses." When the man smiled at her, Anna felt it in the pit of her stomach.

The man, who had started all the problems with August, intrigued Anna. She decided to try to get to know him better. Nothing would come of it, but he did seem to be interesting. She had never been one to flirt, but there could be a first time for everything. *We'll see what August thinks of that!*

"What did you have in mind?" Anna should have been asking the girl, but she turned toward the man.

Although he smiled at her, it didn't reach his eyes. They were piercing, intense, with some secret hidden in their depths. "Whatever Rissa wants is all right with me. She knows what she likes."

Anna took Rissa to the counter where several fashion magazines were stacked. While the girl leafed through the pages, Anna often glanced toward the man. Every time she saw him, his gaze was on her. Soon she began to feel uncomfortable. No man had ever concentrated on her for such a long time.

"I want to have four summer outfits made." Rissa drew Anna's attention from her father. Anna glanced down at the magazine she had open. "I like this dress." She turned the pages to show Anna two more styles. Then she waved a hand toward the summer frock on the dress form in the window. "Can you make that style in my size?"

"Of course." Anna had taken a tablet from under the counter. She wrote down the page number in the magazine. Then she added the style from the window. "You need to pick out what fabrics you want us to use."

"Do you need me to help you?" Gerda stepped through the door.

Anna turned toward her. "I'll let you help Rissa choose her fabrics, and I'll talk to her father about the costs involved."

The man raised one eyebrow at Anna's words. "Oh, it doesn't matter how much they cost. I want Rissa to have what she desires. We can afford it." A mocking smile crossed his face.

"I didn't doubt that for a minute." Anna smiled at him then.

While Gerda and Rissa continued to look through the stacks of fabric, Mr. Le Blanc started asking Anna about the town of Litchfield. The conversation was a pleasant one, but after the Le Blancs left the store, Anna realized that she hadn't found out anything about them. And once again, Mr. Le Blanc kissed her hand before he left the store. His gallantry was a pleasant change from what Anna was used to, but she liked the kiss from August better, even if it hadn't meant anything to him. Strong emotion had been the reason for it, even if it was the wrong emotion.

❧

August was across the street and one block down before he turned to look back at the store. That's when he noticed that the Le Blancs were in the Dress Emporium. He wanted to go back but knew he had no reason to go into the women's store. Maybe he should go to the mercantile. Surely there was something he needed to pick up.

When August entered the establishment, he was glad to see that both Johan and Marja were busy with other customers. He casually made his way to the side of the store nearest the dress shop. He browsed through the merchandise while keeping a close eye on what was transpiring in the next room.

He didn't like the way that man looked at Anna. When she was busy with his daughter, his eyes raked Anna from the top of her head to her feet. And he spent too long on specific parts of her body. August's blood began to simmer. The nerve of that man.

August wished that he hadn't made such a fool of himself earlier with Anna. He knew that she wouldn't listen to a thing he said about that snake oil salesman. A man like him had to be planning some kind of scam. August decided to keep a close watch on him.

Over the next three weeks, Mr. Le Blanc and his daughter insinuated themselves into Litchfield society. They attended church every Sunday. August noticed that they were always slightly late, and when they arrived, they didn't slip in quietly. Everyone in the room knew when they arrived. They invited key people to small *soirees,* as Rissa called them, in their hotel suite. Everyone who was invited was someone important—such as the mayor, the banker, the sheriff, the stationmaster, and the owner of the hotel.

Unfortunately, since Anna and Gerda were business owners, they were often included in the festivities, especially Anna. However, although he was the owner of a business, August was never invited. Neither were Hank or any of the farmers. Only people Le Blanc thought had quite a bit of money. . .and Anna.

When the parties were held downstairs in the hotel, August was able to keep an eye on the proceedings. But when they were in the sitting room of the Le Blancs' hotel suite, he could only guess what went on. What August observed didn't make him change his mind about the man. Something wasn't quite right about him.

❧

The Dress Emporium had received a new shipment of fabrics, and Anna was arranging them on the shelves when August arrived. He came into the shop and leaned on the counter.

"I've come to apologize to you."

Although Anna kept her back to him, she was aware of his every move. She had tried to stay out of his way ever since that unfortunate kiss. Now here he was only a few feet from her. So close she could feel the heat emanating from him, helping her remember the feel and taste of his lips.

"And what do you have to apologize for?" Anna didn't think her heart could take him saying he was sorry for kissing her. There had been only short periods of time since that fateful day when she didn't remember every nuance of that connection, even though it was brief.

"Anna, please look at me." When she turned around and their gazes connected, he continued. "I'm sorry I was angry when I kissed you."

He hadn't said he was sorry that he kissed her, only that he was angry when he did. That was interesting.

"Why were you angry? I hadn't done anything to upset you." Anna crossed her arms and stood her ground.

He nodded. "You're right. I wasn't angry at you. It was that man."

Anna took a deep breath. "Mr. Le Blanc?"

"Yes." August stepped back from the counter and stuffed his hands into the back pockets of his denim trousers.

❧

"You never have liked him, have you?" Anna's question caught August off guard.

"No, I don't trust the man."

Anna looked as if he had said something bad about her. "What did he do to make you not trust him?"

How could August make her understand? He knew that he was right. The man never looked August in the eyes. He had a smooth way of talking, but when August looked at his eyes, there was no light in them. Only a confidence man talked that smoothly. August had seen them at work on more than one occasion. The man had to be a confidence man, but August had no way to prove it.

"That man is up to no good."

The sound Anna made wasn't very ladylike. "I think you're jealous because you weren't invited to any of the parties."

"Jealous? Of that man? Hardly. . .but he's not honest."

August could tell that Anna was getting exasperated. "He was totally honest with Gerda and me. He spent a lot of money in this store. How can you say he's not honest?" Anna was raising her voice a little more with each word she said.

August did the same. "That man is up to no good. Mark my words. You'll see that soon enough."

Anna came around the counter and stood toe to toe with August, and her finger on his chest punctuated each word. "I can't believe you're so pigheaded. He was kind to me, and I won't let you say bad things about him."

"I've seen the way he looked at you when you didn't notice. He was devouring you with his eyes in a very unsavory manner. No decent woman would want a man looking at her like that." August knew that he was shouting, but he couldn't stop himself.

Anna turned and marched to the door of the workroom. There she whirled around. "I can't believe you would stoop so low as to say something like that. I guess you'll be glad to know that he and his daughter left town this morning after picking up the dresses we made for her. We'll probably never see them again." When Anna went through the door, she slammed it shut behind her. The sound reverberated off all four walls of the store.

August stood there stunned. He had done it again. Lost his temper with Anna. What in the world was wrong with him?

❧

Thankfully, it was time to close the shop. When August walked out, Anna came from the workroom and locked the door to the mercantile. She grabbed her coat, gloves, and handbag and hurried out the front door. She didn't want to cry until she got in the apartment, but it took every ounce of strength she had to hold the tears inside. After fumbling with the lock and key, she finally secured the front door.

When Anna closed the apartment door behind her, her reserves were gone. She dropped into the rocking chair and covered her face with her hands. The tears she had been holding back came in a flood, as if a dam inside her had broken. With a keening wail, she rocked and sobbed. Why had God done this to her?

That's where Gerda found her when she returned home, rocking and crying. Anna wished that she had thought about going to her own bedroom. Maybe then Gerda wouldn't have been so concerned about her.

"Anna!" Gerda dropped the bags she was carrying and hurried to the rocking chair. She knelt on the oval braided rug and took Anna's hands in hers. "What happened?"

Anna had carried this load too long by herself. She was tired. Without thinking, the words tumbled out.

"August is angry with me. . .and he doesn't like Mr. Le Blanc. . .and he yelled at me, and—"

"Who yelled at you? Mr. Le Blanc?"

"No, August yelled at me, and he was angry when he kissed me, and—"

Gerda stood up and put her hands on her hips. "August kissed you again?"

"No!" Anna knew that her thoughts were jumbled, and what she was saying didn't make much sense.

Gerda pulled Anna up from the chair and wrapped her arms around her friend. After hugging her for a moment, she led Anna to the settee where they both sat down. Then Gerda began to pray.

"Fader Gud, Anna is upset. Please bring a peace and calmness to her, so we can discuss what is bothering her. Give us wisdom as we try to discern Your will in the matter. In Jesus' name, amen."

Inexplicably, Anna felt a calmness descend upon her. After sitting still for a short time, her thoughts began to make sense.

"Now, Anna," Gerda said. "Start at the beginning, and tell me what's wrong."

Anna stood up and removed her coat while she explained what had happened in the store earlier with August. Gerda sat quietly and listened.

"I think maybe August is jealous of the attention that Mr. Le Blanc is giving you."

That was a new thought to Anna. August jealous? Why would he be jealous?

"Haven't you noticed how attentive he is to you?" Gerda asked.

Anna hadn't thought of August as being attentive to her. He was only a good friend, wasn't he? "Why do you think he's paying any attention to me?" Anna sat down again and clasped her hands in her lap.

"Oh, Anna." Gerda put her hand over Anna's. "I've suspected for some time that August is interested in you. Before Mr. Le Blanc came, I even thought you might be interested in him. Now I'm not sure."

Anna sat for a moment, deep in thought. Then she stood, walked across the room, and looked out the window, staring at nothing in particular. "I can't let myself think about a man that way."

"Why not?" Gerda came to stand beside her. "Every woman looks forward to marriage someday."

Anna looked at Gerda with a stricken expression on her face. "That's not God's plan for me."

Gerda put her hands on her hips. "Why do you say that?"

Anna took a deep breath. Gerda had been her best friend long before they were partners in the business. If she couldn't tell her, who could she tell? Maybe Gerda's prayers would help her accept what was happening to her.

"I don't know when it started, but I do know that there is something wrong with me. Something that keeps a man from loving me enough." For a moment, the words hung in the air between them.

"Anna, how can you say that?" Gerda pulled Anna into her arms and patted her back. "Nothing's wrong with you."

"Gustaf couldn't love me enough. . .even though we were together for years." Anna tried to speak the words evenly, but her voice had a catch in it.

"You know that Olina was the right woman for him, don't you?"

Anna nodded. "Olaf didn't love me enough either. I knew that he shouldn't go on the hunting trip. I begged him not to go. . .if he loved me. He went anyway, not even considering my feelings."

Gerda dropped onto the settee. "I'm so sorry, Anna. I didn't know. But that doesn't mean that something is wrong with you. He wasn't the right man to love you the way God wants you loved."

"If you say so." Anna wasn't convinced. She walked over to the table by the rocking chair and started straightening the doily on top.

Gerda went to her bedroom and returned with her Bible.

She opened it and searched for a particular passage. "I want to read something to you. I read it last night, and God brought it back to my mind. Here it is, Matthew 10:29–31: 'Are not two sparrows sold for a farthing? and one of them shall not fall on the ground without your Father. But the very hairs of your head are all numbered. Fear ye not therefore, ye are of more value than many sparrows.' God made you special, Anna, and He has a plan for you. Maybe you haven't found it yet."

"Read those words to me again." Anna dropped into the rocking chair, leaned her head against the back, and closed her eyes.

After Gerda finished reading the verses, Anna sat and let them soak into her heart.

Gerda began to turn the pages in her Bible again. "Here's another Scripture. Psalm 139:13–16: 'For thou hast possessed my reins: thou hast covered me in my mother's womb. I will praise thee; for I am fearfully and wonderfully made: marvelous are thy works; and that my soul knoweth right well. My substance was not hid from thee, when I was made in secret, and curiously wrought in the lowest parts of the earth. Thine eyes did see my substance, yet being unperfect; and in thy book all my members were written, which in continuance were fashioned, when as yet there was none of them.' Anna, these words apply to you, too. You were fearfully and wonderfully made according to God's plan. You are altogether lovely, as He created you to be. Nothing is wrong with you. And He cares about everything that happens in your life. He understands your desires to have a husband and children, and in His timing, He will bring it about."

These added words were a balm to the wounds in Anna's heart. When Gerda began to pray for her, she sat and listened. She felt the presence of the Lord stronger than she had in a long time, and the pain in her heart started to recede.

eleven

August was glad that he needed to make horseshoes today. While he pounded the red-hot iron bar flat, he berated himself. "Why were you so stupid?" *Bang. . .bang.* "How could you have yelled at Anna?" *Bang. . .bang.* "She'll never know that you love her."

"You're right about that." August hadn't noticed that Gustaf had walked into the blacksmith shop until he spoke above the pounding.

August dropped his chin against his chest and took a deep breath before turning to face his brother. "I guess you heard every word I said." It was a statement, not a question.

"You weren't exactly speaking softly." Gustaf had a twinkle in his eye that August didn't want to see. "I'm surprised that everyone couldn't hear you. It's a good thing the smithy is on the edge of town."

August knew the fiery forge caused his face to redden, but now there was an additional reason. He hoped that no one passing in the street heard what he said.

"There wasn't anyone walking by." Gustaf must have read August's thoughts. He often did that. Sometimes August didn't mind, but more often than not, it drove him crazy.

"Good." August nodded. "So what brings you here today?" He glanced toward the table where he kept things waiting to be repaired. He didn't see anything added to the carefully arranged items already there. "You didn't bring me any work, did you?"

Gustaf slid his hands into his back pockets and rocked up

on the balls of his feet. August knew he did that when he wanted to discuss something serious.

"No, I only thought that you might need someone to talk to."

"Because of what I was saying when you came in?" August studied his brother's expression, trying to discern what he was concerned about.

"No, Gerda talked to me about what happened in the Dress Emporium yesterday."

August stared at the floor. He scuffed the dirt with the toe of his boot, drawing overlapping ovals. "I'm not very proud of that."

"You shouldn't be," Gustaf quickly agreed. "Can you take a break, or do you have too much work?" He glanced around the shop.

August looked at the nearly empty table. "Nothing that I need to rush to finish. Where do you want to talk?" Since there were no chairs in the smithy, it wasn't conducive to long conversations.

"The church worked really well last time. Do you want to go there?"

The brothers were each lost in their own thoughts as they trudged to the church. When they were inside the building, Gustaf led the way to the front pew. After sitting, he bowed his head. August knew his brother was praying. He wanted to pray, too, but instead he sat silently, hoping the feeling of peace he always received at church would soak into him today. However, it seemed to be far away.

Gustaf spoke first. "You're still having trouble with jealousy, aren't you?"

"I don't feel the strong jealousy of you that poisoned my life before." August leaned his forearms on his thighs and let his huge hands dangle between his knees. He studied the wooden floor between his work boots. "It's been coming out about other things now."

"That isn't healthy."

August nodded. "I know. That's why I was berating myself when you came into the smithy."

"Maybe we didn't do enough when we talked last time. I've been reading about roots of bitterness." Light pouring through the one stained glass window cast a warm, multicolored glow over Gustaf's face. "You have to get to the very bottom of them before you can dig them out of your life. Maybe we need to find the root of the jealousy in your heart."

That made sense to August. He sat up and put his arms along the back of the handmade wooden pew, drumming his fingers on the polished surface. "Do you have any idea how I can do that?" He would welcome any help he could get. He had wrestled with this problem far too long.

Gustaf sat silent so long that August thought he wasn't going to answer. "I've been praying about that ever since Gerda told me what happened yesterday. I feel the Lord is telling me that we need to go as far back in your memory as we can. You told me you were jealous of me before we came to America. Do you know how long you felt that jealousy in Sweden?"

For several minutes, August studied the wooden cross that hung behind the pulpit. His thoughts returned to their native land and the life they lived there. "I don't remember ever not being jealous. . .of you."

Gustaf stood and paced toward the platform, but he didn't step up on it. He turned around to face August. "Were you jealous when you were. . .say, ten years old?"

August thought a few minutes while he reconstructed in his mind what he felt when he was ten. "Yes."

"What about when Gerda was born?"

August remembered that Gustaf got to hold their baby sister more often than he did. That had never seemed fair to him. He nodded. "Yes."

"Okay, before that. . . What about when Lars was born?"

It took August awhile, but he remembered when Lars was a baby. Gustaf had been very proud of the new little brother. Suddenly, August could see with clarity into his long-ago memories.

Before Lars was born, Gustaf had doted on August. As the little brother, August had followed him around like a puppy, and his older brother was proud of him. He helped him do a lot of things. They were real buddies, always together. August could hear his father's voice saying how his two boys were inseparable and how proud he was of them. August didn't feel anything but admiration for his big brother. He was stunned. It took him awhile before he could articulate what God had revealed to him.

He finally looked up at Gustaf, his beloved older brother. "I was not jealous of you before Lars was born." He hated to admit that. What would Gustaf think of him now, knowing that jealousy of a baby brother had caused all the heartache?

Gustaf smiled. "I'm so glad. I was afraid we wouldn't be able to find the root of your jealousy. I've prayed since yesterday that God would reveal it to one of us. He answered my prayers. I praise Him for that."

August looked up at the ceiling. "I remember that you were so proud of me. We went everywhere together. Fader even told people how proud he was of his two sons." He dropped his head and studied the floorboards. "Then when Lars was born, you didn't spend as much time with me." The words sounded so petty coming from his mouth.

Gustaf moved to sit beside August on the pew. "Brother, I'm so sorry that I caused this."

August looked up at him. "You were only a boy. You didn't do anything any other brother wouldn't."

Gustaf put his arm across August's shoulders. "I think it'll help if I ask for your forgiveness, and you choose to freely give it to me."

August had tears in his own eyes when he looked into his brother's teary eyes. "Of course I forgive you. I. . ." He cleared his throat before he could continue. ". . .love you."

The brothers clutched each other in a strong embrace while they wept for the special times they had lost. When they finally stood, each pulled a bandanna from his pocket and wiped his face. August couldn't believe how much lighter he felt. It was as if the weight of an anvil had been lifted from his heart.

"This was a turning point in my life." August smiled at Gustaf. "Thank you for helping me."

"Jealousy has been a habit in your life a long time, but I believe God will help you break it, if you let Him."

When the two men returned to the blacksmith shop, they both walked with a spring in their steps. August expected Gustaf to leave when they reached his horse that was tied to the hitching post outside the building, but instead he came into the smithy.

After leaning against the table, Gustaf crossed his arms over his chest. "So, what are you going to do about Anna?"

August didn't have a ready answer. He had been wondering the same thing. What could he do about Anna? After yesterday, she probably thought he was a lunatic, or worse.

"I don't know." He started straightening things on the table, even though they weren't in disarray.

"Do you love her?"

August stopped what he was doing and faced his brother. "You get right to the heart of the matter, don't you?"

Gustaf didn't say a word but gave August time to consider his answer.

August leaned against the table beside his brother and crossed his own arms. "Yes, I love her, for all the good it'll do me."

"Does she know?"

After thinking a minute, August said, "She ought to."

Gustaf blew out an exasperated breath. "Why should she? Have you told her?"

"Of course not, but I've been showing her in a lot of ways."

"What kind of ways?"

August started listing them. "I've made them a cushioned sewing chair. I bought a book of poetry for the apartment. I try to fix everything that needs fixing. I go to see her almost every day."

Gustaf straightened away from the table and brushed off the back of his jeans. "You have a lot to learn about women, Brother. None of that was for only Anna. Gerda shared them."

"Well, I did buy her some pretty handkerchiefs. They had dainty needlework flowers on them. They reminded me of her when I saw them in the mercantile. On impulse, I bought them and took them to her."

Gustaf smiled. "That's a step in the right direction. Now stop doing things that can be for both Gerda and Anna. Make sure that everything you do to show her you love her is for Anna alone. And eventually, you'll need to tell her how you feel."

"I kissed her."

Gustaf laughed. "Oh, I heard about that kiss. Remember, Gerda was there. I don't think that one counts. You probably need to do something to make her forget that one. A while back, didn't you tell me that you were going to pray about whether Anna was the woman God wanted you to marry?"

August moved away from the table. "Yes, and I feel that God told me she was. That's why I've been trying to do things for her. So she would start having feelings for me."

"If God has told you she's the one, pour all your efforts into wooing her." Gustaf headed out the door, but he turned back. "You're not getting any younger, you know."

❧

After her conversation with Gerda, Anna couldn't get August out of her mind. Was he as interested in her as Gerda thought? If so, why did he yell at her? Wouldn't a man who loved her want to protect her, not yell at her?

Protect her? That was an idea. Maybe August thought he was protecting her from Pierre. . .Mr. Le Blanc. The words that August said about the way Mr. Le Blanc looked at her left an uncomfortable feeling in Anna's heart. She had allowed the man to become a friend. Had he been unsuitable? If so, why hadn't she noticed? Besides, she wouldn't even have paid any attention to him if it hadn't been for August's irrational accusations when the Le Blancs first came to town.

Anna didn't need all this turmoil in her life. If August was interested in her, he needed to learn how to treat a woman. And it wasn't by yelling at her in her own store. Anna hoped there weren't many customers in the mercantile. She was sure that whoever was there heard every word she and August exchanged. Anna hadn't even been able to face Marja or Johan since the confrontation.

August hadn't been showing interest in her. He had been trying to control her, telling her what to do. She didn't need that. It reminded her too much of the last words Olaf spoke to her before he left on that hunting trip. Anna didn't want a man who controlled her without taking into consideration what she felt about anything. She wanted one who would love her the way her father loved her mother. He was the head of the household, but he wasn't heavy-handed about it. If Anna were to marry, she would be glad to be a helpmeet, as the Bible said, to a man who wasn't overbearing.

Too much had happened in the last few days. Anna was tired of all the turmoil. The best thing for her to do would be to stay out of the way when August was around. Then he couldn't yell at her again.

❧

After his conversation with Gustaf, August plotted his next move. He would win Anna's love or die trying. She was worth it. He could face anything with her by his side. And the family they would have would be such a blessing.

The next time he went to the dress shop, Anna wasn't there. Gerda said that she had left for a few minutes. So he decided to come back later. Once again, Anna had left before he got there. August went into the mercantile to look at the newer merchandise. The Braxtons were always adding things to the store. Recently, it was a larger shelf of books. He was browsing through the titles when he heard Anna and Gerda talking in the dress shop.

He picked up a book of poetry by Emily Dickinson. The slim volume was bound in soft, maroon leather. Anna would like it. Gerda had said that Anna enjoyed the book of poetry he bought for the apartment. After paying for the volume, he asked Marja to wrap it up for him. Then he went into the dress shop. Gerda was rearranging some of the merchandise in the showroom.

"August, you've come back." Gerda spoke louder than usual.

He wondered why she spoke so loud, then he heard a door closing. It sounded as if it came from the workroom. When he asked about Anna, Gerda told him that she wasn't in the shop.

As he walked toward the boardinghouse, carrying the package wrapped in brown paper and tied with string, he wondered what was going on. Was Anna hiding from him? Of course, he couldn't blame her. He would have to figure out a way to get her to see him. Maybe he could go to the apartment after dinner and deliver this book.

August finished the delicious meal Mrs. Olson prepared, then he went upstairs and shaved again. He wanted to look as nice as possible when he saw Anna. He even changed into his best pants and shirt. When August started toward the mercantile building, he couldn't see any light in the windows of the apartment. The bedrooms were on the front of the building. Maybe the girls were in the parlor or the kitchen. But when he arrived at the top of the stairs, there wasn't a hint of light coming from the windows. They weren't home. All that trouble for nothing. But that was all right. He would try again tomorrow. August was patient. He would do whatever it took to win Anna's love.

twelve

June

Anna enjoyed poetry. The words sang in her heart. After eating lunch in the apartment, she picked up the book of poetry August brought by two evenings ago. She decided to sit and read a few pages before she returned to the shop so Gerda could have lunch.

When she sat in her favorite rocking chair, instead of opening the volume, her fingers stroked the texture of the smooth surface. She lifted the book close to her face. The scent of the new leather reminded her of August. The other book of poetry he bought had been for both her and Gerda, but this one was inscribed inside from August to her. She would never understand that man. He had aggravated her when he yelled at her. She placed the fingertips of her right hand over her lips, once again feeling the memory of his lips on hers. When he kissed her, it touched more than her mouth. Even in his anger, his lips had felt soft and velvety.

If truth were known, Anna hadn't wanted the kiss to end so quickly. She had often wondered what it would feel like to be kissed on the mouth. Gustaf had never kissed her, and when Olaf did, it was on the cheek or forehead. But August had touched her lips, and she couldn't forget the feeling. He was such a confusing man. Either yelling at her, kissing her, or doing nice things. Maybe all the good things could outweigh the other.

When Anna realized how long she had sat daydreaming, she put the book down and went to the bedroom to check her hair in the mirror over her washstand. Gerda had waited long enough for her lunch.

❧

August had the doors of the smithy wide open. It was June, and the heat from the forge called for a cool breeze. But this spring had been pretty dry. He would welcome a storm if it brought the wind to cool things off.

For some reason, today the forge smelled hotter, more smoky. August went to the door to get a whiff of fresh air. When he stepped outside, he realized that the smell of fire and smoke didn't only come from the forge. The livery stable that was a little ways down the street had smoke pouring out through the door and every window. It billowed from the opening to the hay loft and formed a wreath around the entire roof of the building.

Fire!

August wondered about the proprietor, but Hank stepped from the inferno, leading two horses. So August ran as fast as he could toward the fire bell. By the time he reached the bell, Hank had tied those two horses to hitching posts and headed back toward the stable. August pulled the rope hard several times until people carrying buckets started running down the street toward him. They would form a bucket brigade, dipping water from Lake Ripley. It was a good thing the livery was at the edge of town, near the body of water.

In other circumstances, they would have used the fire wagon. The trouble was that both the wagon and the horses that pulled it were kept in the livery. It was too late to get to the wagon, but Hank was leading the fire horses from the burning barn when August returned.

❧

Gerda and Anna were working on a wedding dress that a customer needed by the end of the week. After they had sold Anna's wedding dress soon after the Dress Emporium opened, many brides ordered their gowns from them. Anna had finished sewing the last seam on the machine when the fire bell startled them. They both ran out on the sidewalk to see what was happening. They were appalled by what they saw.

"What do you think we should do?" Gerda shaded her eyes with one hand. "They need help with the bucket brigade."

"Most of the town is heading that way, but if we both go, we'll never finish this dress in time. I wouldn't want to disappoint the bride, would you?"

Gerda nodded. "You're right. At least I can pray while I work on it. Be sure to come back as soon as you can and let me know what is happening."

Anna left Gerda in the workroom, grabbed a bucket, and hurried to join the brigade from the lake. While she ran, she searched the sky for even a hint of a cloud. Rain would be especially welcome right now. It could do more than any bucket brigade to put the fire out.

When she reached the line of people, she looked toward the lake. There were fifty or more people passing full buckets one way and empty buckets back. Her brother Ollie let her get in line in front of him. He was near the end of the brigade closest to the livery. She would be able to see all that was happening.

Anna handed her empty bucket to Ollie and took the full one he was passing forward. Then she exchanged buckets with the person in front of her. By the time she turned back to Ollie, he held another full bucket. Even though the work was repetitious, it allowed her the opportunity to watch

August without him being aware of it.

When she ran to get in line, she noticed that August was the one who rang the fire bell. She watched him go to some of the horses tied along the street and try to calm them.

It was so like August to care for the animals. Probably that was one reason he wanted to be a blacksmith. He knew how important it was for animals to be treated right. Anna had heard several men say that his horseshoes were some of the best, and they complimented August on treating the animals with care while he shod them. It was another thing to like about him. Too bad he was so bossy with her.

While she was watching him, August looked her way. She turned around, intent on passing the buckets quickly. When she glanced at him again, he was headed toward the owner of the livery stable.

❧

"Are all the horses out?" August called to Hank.

"No. There's one more. I've tied all the others to hitching posts." He pointed down the street where August had been trying to calm down the skittish horses that were dancing around, pulling on their leads.

August knew that horses didn't like fire or smoke. It might take a lot to calm them. He wished he could help them, but right now, the fire was more important. The livery building was wooden and filled with so many things that burned easily. Hay fueled the flames, sending them higher and higher. They had broken through the roof by the time August neared the building. Sparkling embers danced in the air above the fire. At least there wasn't any wind to blow them toward the other wooden buildings.

Although the buckets were being passed from hand to hand at a fast clip, the small amount of water poured on the raging fire didn't seem to affect it at all. August started toward the open doorway of the stable.

❧

"Hey, you can't go in there!"

Anna heard the shout about someone going into the building, and she looked toward the livery. Who was that man walking so close to the inferno?

"There's still one horse inside!"

Right after August's shouted statement, the shrill whinny of a scared animal pierced the air. To Anna's horror, August continued toward the raging fire. In an instant, he was swallowed up in the roiling smoke.

"No!" She couldn't leave the line, but she wanted to.

The thump of her heartbeat in her throat almost choked her. August, dear August. For the first time, she realized that she truly loved him. And it might be too late. She might never get the chance to tell him. What he was doing was heroic, but it was also stupid. Who in his right mind would rush into a burning building? But Anna knew his tender heart made him want to rescue the frightened animal. She began to pray frantically that his efforts wouldn't be in vain. She begged God to bring both August and the horse out of the inferno.

❧

August pulled the blue bandanna from his hip pocket and tied it around his face, leaving only his eyes uncovered. If he wanted to find the horse, he needed to see. Before he entered the stable, he should have asked Hank which stall the horse was in, but he couldn't go back now. The overpowering heat almost brought August to his knees, but he heard the animal's horrible scream again. The sound gave him a direction to go.

Thick smoke obscured most of the things around him. He stumbled over burning pieces of wood that had fallen from the beams. He didn't know how much time was left before the roof would cave in. Flames licked upward on the sides of the walls and scrabbled across the floor. August stamped the flickers near his feet, keeping them at bay for a short time. At least he had on heavy boots.

One more agonized cry from the animal brought August to his stall. The horse was so overcome with fear that August had a hard time catching hold of its bridle, which, thankfully, someone had left on the animal. He grabbed the lead line that lay across the stall divider. He attached it to the bridle and tried to lead the horse toward the door.

When the animal refused to move from its stall, August pulled the bandanna from his own face and quickly covered the horse's eyes. Then he jerked on the lead line and moved as swiftly as possible toward the stable doors. August knew that if he didn't get there very soon, neither he nor the animal would survive. The air was full of burning bits of debris that were constantly falling through the thick haze.

Smoke and heat seared August's lungs, so he tried to hold his breath. Choking and coughing, he stumbled forward pulling the horse as hard as he could. *Oh, Gud, please help us. Let us reach the door in time.*

❧

Anna stood horrified, as did many others in the brigade. She held her breath for what seemed an eternity, crying out to God to save August. Finally, the majestic animal and man came through the smoke-filled opening. August stumbled and fell to his knees. With a shrill cry, the horse reared up on his hind legs and pulled his lead away from August. The bandanna fell from its head, and the horse shot away from the heat and smoke. Hank ran toward one of the other horses and jumped on its back. He took off after the runaway. Anna knew that he wanted to bring it back safely.

When Anna looked back toward August, he was lying on the ground, much too close to the burning building. She passed off the bucket she held, gathered her skirt with both hands, and started running toward him.

One of the men tried to stop her, but she pushed past him. It took three men to hold her and keep her from rushing into danger.

"Stop! We have two men going to get him!" It took awhile for the words to soak into Anna's fear-crazed brain. Finally, she stopped writhing and twisting, trying to get away from the hands that held her.

"He has to be all right! He just has to!" Then she burst into tears.

Gustaf and Ollie ran toward August's still form. Anna was thankful for brothers. They would take care of August. She wondered where Lowell was. When she glanced around looking for him, he was coming from the direction of the doctor's office. Carrying his black bag, Dr. Bradley hurried after Lowell.

❧

August couldn't remember when breathing had hurt so much. Not even the time the plow horse kicked him when he was only ten years old. It was agony to take a breath. He tasted smoke and flames. He smelled smoke and flames. The only way to get a breath was to cough some of the smoke out of his lungs. When he did, he sputtered, trying not to scream from the pain.

Finally aware that two men were carrying him, he tried to open his eyes, but even that was hard. When he glimpsed Ollie and Gustaf, he relaxed as much as he could without becoming dead weight to them.

Lowell and Dr. Bradley met them in the middle of the

street. The doctor told the two men to lower August to the dusty ground. People gathered close around, and August felt as if he couldn't breathe at all.

"All right now!" Doc's voice thundered. "Everybody back! Give the man some air!"

When people moved back, it brought some relief, but not much. Doc's hands roved over his form, seeking, searching. Doc put a stethoscope against August's chest and listened.

"He doesn't seem to have any burns on his body. He's just breathed in too much smoke."

"What can we do to help him?" August was glad his brother asked the question that was screaming in his mind. "Should I take him out to the farm?"

August glanced at Doc in time to see him shake his head. "I would like to have him here in town so I can keep an eye on him."

"I don't feel good about taking him to the boardinghouse. There wouldn't be anyone to look after him," Gustaf said.

"You can take him to the apartment."

Anna had come to stand by Lowell. The sound of her voice was a soothing balm to August's heart. He tried to smile at her but didn't think she noticed. She was intent on her conversation with the doctor.

"That's a good idea," Gustaf agreed. "I'll go get *Moder*. She'll want to take care of him."

thirteen

Anna rushed to the Dress Emporium and burst through the front door. "Gerda, August has been hurt!"

Gerda placed the wedding dress she was hemming on the cutting table and hurried into the shop, toward her best friend. "How bad is he?"

So she could catch her breath, Anna stopped beside the counter and leaned one hand on it, placing the other over her heart. "I don't think he's burned, but he went into the livery stable to rescue a trapped horse. When they came out, August fainted." Anna had never swooned in her life, but she felt as if she could crumple into a heap right now.

Gerda put the fingers of her right hand over her mouth, and tears started making their way down her cheeks. After she sobbed a moment, she took a deep breath and asked, "Is he going to be all right?"

Tears were also streaming down Anna's cheeks, and she didn't even try to wipe them off. "Lowell went to get the doctor. Doc wants August to stay in town. I told them they could bring him to the apartment. I hope that's all right with you."

Gerda grabbed Anna and held her tight. "Of course, I want him here. I want to take care of him."

Anna clutched her also. "Gustaf has already gone to get your mother. Lowell and Ollie will bring August to our place."

The two young women decided to close the dress shop. If anyone needed anything, they could come back later. Everyone in town would understand.

Lowell and Ollie met them at the bottom of the outside stairs. Their shoulders supported August's arms, and he was trying to walk, even though the other two men carried most of his weight. That was probably why it had taken this long for them to arrive.

The two women preceded them up the steps, and Gerda immediately went into her own room to prepare the bed for her brother. Anna stood by the door and watched, feeling helpless, while her brothers helped August across the parlor and down the short hall to the bedroom. Before she shut the outside door, Dr. Bradley reached the top of the stairs.

After showing the doctor to Gerda's bedroom, Anna dropped into her rocker. Unmoving, she stared unseeing at her hands that were clasped in her lap. It was hard waiting for the doctor to finish tending to August.

Lowell and Ollie soon joined her in the parlor. They didn't sit. Instead they prowled around as if they couldn't settle down. Anna knew they were probably as worried as she was.

She glanced up at them. "Has Doc almost finished with August?"

Lowell continued to pace the room, but Ollie dropped onto the settee across from her. "He was still working with him when we came out."

"Did he say anything about how badly August is hurt?"

Before he could answer, Gerda came down the hall and joined them. "Dr. Bradley said that he would talk to us when he's finished, but he was sure that August would recover."

Anna let out the breath she hadn't even realized she was holding. August would be all right.

Lowell and Ollie decided to go back and join the battle against the fire. Although the livery stable was a total loss, the townspeople were still trying to make sure the fire didn't spread to any other structures. All buildings in the vicinity were also wooden and could easily burn.

Gerda went to the kitchen while Anna continued to sit in her rocker. She remembered how she felt when she saw August run into the burning building. Love had welled up and overtaken her completely. She wanted, more than anything, to be able to express that love. But Anna knew that she had had strong feelings twice before. She began to wonder if she could trust her emotions. Nothing she experienced had led to a lasting relationship. Maybe this new love wasn't strong enough either. Anna felt confused, but she didn't want to completely let go of these feelings. They seemed to be different from before, but she couldn't be sure. Life—or was that love—was much too confusing.

❧

By the time Dr. Bradley had finished with his thorough examination, August was exhausted. He had been having such a hard time breathing, and Doc said that was making him even more tired. Unfortunately, there wasn't much Doc could do for August. He said it would take time for all the smoke to get out of his lungs. Until then, he wanted August to take it easy.

"I'll make sure he does." Ingrid Nilsson stepped through the door just as the doctor made that statement.

August was glad to see his mother, even though he hadn't wanted to bother her. He tried to smile, hoping it didn't look like a grimace. Although he didn't have any blisters on his skin—and that was a surprise—it felt as if he had worked two days in the sun without any shade. His skin was tight and dry. He was sure that if he could see in Gerda's mirror, he would be red, too. If he smiled too much, his face might crack.

"Now, Doctor, what do I need to do to help my son?"

Dr. Bradley smiled. "I'm glad you're here, Mrs. Nilsson. I know you'll take good care of him."

August knew his mother. She always wrote everything down. She took a small tablet and pencil out of her handbag and wrote down everything the doctor told her. *Moder* was careful like that.

"Keep the windows open, so he has fresh air to breathe. If anyone has time, have them fan him. That will help move the air from the windows to where he is in the bed. You might even send over to the ice house and get him some ice. Chip small pieces off the block for him to eat. That should help him start to cool down." Doc turned and looked at August. "And make sure he drinks a lot of liquid. He's probably pretty dry after being in that fire. It was like a giant oven."

When August's mother turned her attention from the doctor to her son, she asked another question. "And what should I do for his skin? It's awfully red and dry."

"Any kind of lotion you have would be good. Or if you don't have any, use butter or lard. But be careful when you are smearing it on him so you don't damage his skin any more than it already is."

Well, great! August couldn't help thinking about Anna being in the same apartment. *I'm going to look like a greased pig. That should really make her love me.*

❧

Soon after the doctor left, Johan and Marja Braxton arrived at the top of the stairs. When Anna opened the door, she was surprised. Both of them carried folding cots.

"We thought you might need these for tonight." Marja put her cot down and leaned it against the wall beside the door. She took Johan's from him, and he left. "I knew that with two extra people up here, you need a place for them to sleep."

Anna thanked her. "We'll put one in my bedroom and the other in Gerda's. That's where August is. He probably needs someone in there with him all night."

Mrs. Nilsson came out of Gerda's bedroom. "Marja, how nice to see you."

Marja handed Ingrid a small tin. "Here's some salve. We've had good results using it on burns. Maybe it will help August."

"Thank you." Mrs. Nilsson hugged her friend.

"Another thing we've done when someone has a burn is put mint compresses on it. The herb has a cooling effect. Johan is going over to the garden to pull some of mine. He'll bring it up here for you."

Ingrid smiled. "How thoughtful you are, Marja."

"The women at the church want to help, too, so they've made a list of people who will bring meals to you the next few days."

Anna was surprised. "There are three women here. We could take care of the cooking."

Marja turned toward her. "We know you can." She put her hand on Anna's arm. "But August is always so helpful to everyone else. This is a way to show how much we love him."

All Anna could do was nod, because her throat was tight, and her eyes were full of tears.

❧

How long was he going to have to stay in this room? August was tired of the confinement, even though it had only been three days. He sat up on the side of the bed. He had to sit there for a few moments. All this inactivity would make any man feel a little woozy. Of course, the fire had sapped his strength, too. While he waited for his head to clear, he flexed his stiff hands. The blaze had left them dry, cracked, and sore.

He was glad that no one had taken away his clothes. He reached across to the chair and got his trousers. After carefully pulling them on, he stood up, walked to the window, and leaned both hands against the facing. His gaze swept up and down the street. There was a lot of activity outside. That was good. Everything was back to normal. At the end of the street, he could barely make out the pile of burned-out rubble that used to be the livery stable. At least nothing else burned.

When Gustaf came to see him the day after the incident, he told August that he had banked the fire in the forge and closed up the smithy. August was thankful to have such a thoughtful brother. How could he have let petty, childish jealousy rob him of the close relationship they should have enjoyed all those years? He was thankful that God had helped them overcome that obstacle.

Over the last few days, August often questioned his own sanity. *What kind of idiot runs into a burning building?* But then the memory of the agonized cry of the crazed animal rang through his head, and he answered his own question. The kind of idiot that he was, and he would do it again without a moment's hesitation. The best thing about all that happened was that not a single animal was destroyed in the fire, or even injured.

His mother, sister, and Anna had been taking care of him. The ice soothed his throat those first two days, and the salve that the Braxtons contributed helped his skin, even though it didn't smell very good. The mint compresses had been the most pleasant part of the treatment. At least they hadn't used butter or lard on him. He had been spared that indignity.

The three women had taken turns fanning him. When one would tire, another would take her place. There hadn't been much talking during that time. His throat hurt too much.

Besides, Doc had suggested that he give his voice a rest.

Lying there covered up to his chin with a sheet, August had loved Anna with his eyes. The only problem was that she didn't look straight at him when she was in the room. She would sit and fan the fresh air toward him. Sometimes, she even read to him from the Bible or that book of poetry he bought her. The sound of her voice was music to his ears—and his heart. Then she would relinquish her place to his mother or sister. They never left Anna in the room alone with him more than a few minutes.

Why was Anna so aloof?

"What are you doing up?" Gerda tried to help August back to bed, but he shook her hands off.

"I'm not an invalid. I need to move around to keep up my strength. I'll be going back to work soon."

Gerda put her hands on her hips the same way their mother often did. "Not before Doc says you can."

August dropped onto the side of the bed. "When is he coming again?"

"Later today, I think." Gerda sat in the chair beside him.

"Good. Is Anna working at the Dress Emporium right now?"

He didn't like the look in Gerda's eyes when she answered. "Why do you want to know where Anna is?"

August got up again and walked back to the window. He leaned his left arm against the facing and studied the street again. He didn't want Gerda to read anything in his expression. "I need to talk to you about her."

When he turned back around, Gerda had crossed her arms. "I'm listening."

After August told Gerda how aloof Anna had been, he asked her if she knew of anything he had done to make Anna mad or to hurt her. At first, he thought Gerda wasn't going to answer. She just sat there. Then she bowed her head, and he knew she was praying. He decided to pray, too.

After a period of silent contemplation, Gerda started telling August how worried she was about Anna. She finished by telling him that Anna thought something was wrong with her that kept a man from loving her enough.

"That's the most ridiculous thing I've ever heard. There's nothing wrong with Anna."

"I told her that, but I don't think she believed me, even though I shared Scriptures with her about how special God had created her. At first, I thought she understood, but now I'm not so sure."

That gave August something to think about. When Gerda left to start dinner, he kept mulling over what she had said. He picked up his Bible and asked God to show him how he could help Anna. He was more determined than ever to marry her.

fourteen

When Dr. Bradley came to check on August later that day, he found him sitting in the rocking chair in the parlor of the apartment.

"Doc, I want to go home." August got up and walked toward the door. "And I want to go back to work."

The doctor didn't even examine August this time. He turned toward Ingrid, who had opened the door, and smiled. "I think he's ready."

She nodded and took hold of August's arm with both hands. "I believe you're right." She smiled up at him. "You can't keep a Nilsson man down very long."

August knew that it was probably too late in the day to get much work done. It would take too long to get the forge hot enough. He would start early the next morning. After gathering up all his belongings that had made their way into the apartment, he headed toward the boardinghouse. In one way, he was glad to be out of that apartment. It had almost seemed like a prison to him. But in another way, he would miss seeing Anna so often. He would have to work on ways to accomplish that.

On the way home, he noticed a poster on the front window of the mercantile. The first barn dance of the summer would be Saturday night. Anna liked to dance, so he would ask her to let him escort her to the festivity. He whistled a happy tune the rest of the way to his room.

The next day was Friday, and August only worked until noon. He didn't have many things on his table to finish. As soon as people realized that he was open again, that would change. But he was glad to be able to quit after only five hours. It would take him a little while to build back to his original strength.

After closing the smithy, he went over to the Dress Emporium. Gerda and Anna were in the shop when he arrived.

"How are my two favorite girls today?"

Both of them looked up from their individual tasks when they heard his voice. By their expressions, he could tell that Gerda was glad to see her brother. Anna was a little wary of him. That was all right.

"I came to ask if I could take the two of you to lunch at the hotel. I want to thank you for the use of your apartment."

Anna was quick to answer. "Oh, you don't have to thank us for that."

"I know." August smiled straight into her eyes. "I want to. Please let me do this for you."

❧

Anna couldn't look away from the pull of August's intense gaze. What was it about this man? Everything about him interested her. Those eyes that sometimes looked cloudy and gray were as blue as Lake Ripley. If she wasn't careful, she could drown in their depths. She was glad when he finally looked at his sister, wasn't she?

"What do you say?" he asked.

Anna glanced at Gerda, who was smiling. Anna was trying to think of a kind way to turn him down when she heard Gerda accept for both of them. How could she? Being with August was dangerous to Anna's peace of mind.

When they arrived at the hotel, they were shown to a table by the window. Tantalizing aromas caused Anna's stomach to growl. She was mortified. Now she wished she had eaten a good breakfast. She glanced up and caught a twinkle in August's eyes.

"It's a good thing I came along when I did." He laughed. "I rescued you from dying of hunger."

Anna joined his laughter. The rest of the meal was spent in pleasant banter as they consumed the delicious food. While he escorted them back to the store, Anna realized that she had more fun at lunch than she had experienced in a long time.

After they unlocked the door to the Dress Emporium, Gerda hurried through the shop and opened the door that connected to the mercantile. Then she went into the workroom, leaving Anna and August alone in the display room. Anna started straightening the accessories on the sideboard by the outside wall. She kept her back to August, but she was totally aware of him.

"Thank you for lunch."

When he spoke, his voice came from close behind her. "You're welcome, Anna."

She liked the way he said her name. It sounded different from the way anyone else had ever said it. As if her name was special. She wanted to turn toward him so she could see the expression on his face. But she was afraid to. He was standing much too close.

"I want to ask you something."

The words sounded husky, almost intimate. She wanted to shake that thought out of her head, but if she did, he might think she didn't want him to ask his question.

"What is it, August?" She almost couldn't get the words out.

He stepped back a little, so she turned toward him. He slid his hands into the front pockets of his trousers. She wondered if he was trying to hide his hands. What a silly thought!

"There's a barn dance tomorrow night. Are you going?"

Anna looked up into August's face, studying his expression. "I hadn't planned on it."

He shuffled his feet, as if he was nervous. "I want to go, but not alone. Maybe you could go with me. I know how much you like barn dances." Finally, he smiled.

She had always liked parties. All kinds of parties. She loved being around people, and it had been a long time since she felt like going to a party. Maybe it was time to go again.

"It's okay, Anna. You don't have to go if you don't want to." His voice sounded tender.

"But I do want to go. Thank you for asking me. You're a good friend."

❧

A good friend. Anna had called him a good friend. That was nice, but August wanted so much more than friendship from her. August paced across his room at the boardinghouse and leaned one hand on the window frame. He stared out the window and watched birds flit around in the tops of the trees across the street. Had he only heard what he wanted to when he asked God if Anna was the woman he should share his life with? He was glad that he had time before the party to ask Him once again. After praying a few minutes, he listened very carefully for God's answer. Just as it happened before, he felt that God was telling him yes. So he asked God how to reach her with his love.

It was too bad that the livery stable had burned down. He wanted to rent a nice buggy to take her to the dance. Instead, he had to borrow a vehicle from his brother. Since Gustaf and Olina were also going to the party, they would be using the buggy. So August borrowed the farm wagon.

Before he picked up Anna, he cleaned the wagon as much as he could. He put one of the quilts his mother had given him on the seat to pad it for Anna. He wanted her to be comfortable on the hard wooden bench. He planned to be especially attentive to her at the party. He would look for ways to show his affection for her.

❧

The ride out to the Madsens' farm, where the dance was being held, was pleasant. August kept up a lively conversation with Anna. That in itself was surprising. He was the quiet Nilsson brother, but since he had been coming to the dress shop often, he had been talking more around Anna. She was surprised that she enjoyed the ride so much. Of course the padded seat helped. August had explained about wanting a buggy, and she was impressed by his thoughtfulness. He was a nice man. No wonder her heart was filled with strong emotions toward him. It would be so easy to love him completely, but there was still that question in her mind.

They arrived at the large barn, which was overflowing with the light of the many lanterns hung around the walls, and anticipation filled Anna's heart. It had been too long since she had been to a dance. The musicians were already playing. There were two fiddlers, a banjo player, and one man played a harmonica. A square dance was starting. August pulled Anna into a square that was forming at one end of the barn.

It didn't take long for them to catch up with the other dancers. They moved through the intricate patterns shouted out by the caller. Every time August held her in his arms for a twirl, it seemed to Anna as if he held her a little tighter than anyone else did. When that set was over, Anna felt breathless. . .and warm.

"Let me get you some cider," August whispered in her ear.

He left her sitting on a bale of hay and quickly returned with two cups of the cool liquid. When he sat beside her, their shoulders rested against each other. She liked the feeling of him next to her. A wall of strength. The faint scent of bay rum filled the air and mingled with the aromas of hay, food, and cider.

Before long another farmer asked Anna to be his partner. When she looked at August, he nodded. While that set of square dances continued, Anna often glanced at August. Every time she saw him, he was watching her every move. She thought he would dance with someone else, but he didn't.

The next song was a waltz, and August claimed Anna as his partner. Although they only touched in three places—his hand on the back of her waist, her hand resting on his shoulder, and their other hands clasped—she felt a strong connection between them. For a large man, he moved with a grace that not many men had. He led her smoothly around the floor. She felt as if she were floating on air. Too soon the song ended, and another farmer asked her to share a square dance with him.

As before, August didn't dance with anyone. He sat on a bale of hay and sipped a cup of cider, never taking his eyes from her. Why didn't he dance with someone else, or at least go talk to some other men?

This pattern continued for most of the evening. August danced with Anna about half the time. He asked for all the waltzes and the lively polkas. When they were getting refreshments, he never left her side. While they were together off the dance floor, he carried on conversations with her. But when they waltzed, he whirled her across the floor and seemed to be communicating something to her with his eyes. She wasn't sure what it was.

The only part of the evening that was uncomfortable was when she was with another man. August always agreed to share her company, but while she danced with someone else, he stared at her. The longer this went on, the more Anna's memories of another party surfaced. The evening Gustaf told her he only wanted to be her friend. August had stared at her that night, too. Finally, Anna had all she could take.

❧

August knew something was bothering Anna when she stalked across the floor toward him. She was not smiling. He didn't want everyone to hear whatever she had to say to him.

He stood when she got close. "How about taking a walk in the cool night air with me?"

Anna seemed surprised, but she agreed. He held out his arm. When she rested her hand in the crook, he led her out the door and across the barnyard to a bench that sat under a spreading maple tree. Moonlight illuminated the area, but they were hidden in the shadows. Across the fence that surrounded the pasture, a cow lay in the tall grass. Her calf snuggled close to her, and they were both asleep.

"What's bothering you, my Anna?"

For a moment, the silence was broken only by sounds of the night. In the distance, bullfrogs croaked, and a cow lowed in the pasture. August could tell by the expression on Anna's face that she was surprised by what he said.

She ignored the name he called her and answered the question with one of her own. "Why were you staring at me all evening?"

August was glad that she had been watching him, too. "Ah, Anna, I couldn't help it. Your loveliness is breathtaking."

The comment seemed to make Anna speechless. Then she said, "But you didn't answer my question."

August tried to ignore the excitement that was building inside him. Anna looked down at her hands, which were clasped in her lap. He placed his hand over hers. Above them, the leaves fluttered in the soft breeze, making a whispering sound as they touched.

She turned to look at him. "I was remembering another party when you watched me all evening, too."

He smiled. "And when was that? I've watched you at many parties."

Anna gasped and started to pull her hands out from under his. "It was the night that Gustaf took me home the last time. He told me that he only wanted to be friends."

He slid his arm across her shoulders and searched her face, trying to read her emotions. "And that made you unhappy, didn't it?"

"I loved him. . .and thought he loved me." The words were so quiet that August almost missed them.

Footsteps crunched along the gravel walkway. He glanced to see who was coming, but the person continued on to the house without noticing them under the tree.

"Are you still upset about that night?" August pulled her closer and settled her head against his shoulder. "Later you did plan to marry Olaf."

Anna relaxed in his embrace. "I still love Gustaf, but more like a brother. I know Olina is the woman for him."

August rested his chin on her head, inhaling the sweet fragrance of her hair. He wished he could stay here with her forever.

"Olaf didn't love me enough."

"He wasn't the man for you either." August paused, then continued. "Anna, I would like to court you."

Anna was surprised when August said that. Wasn't he only a friend? Oh, her feelings for him were strong and deep, but were they enough? And would his feelings continue if they courted?

"I'm afraid."

He pulled away and looked at her. "You, Anna? You're strong and fearless."

"But not in the ways of love."

He laughed. "You are a delight to me. *Ja,* that's for sure."

She was confused. "Why do you say that?"

"I've been praying about a relationship with you. I want to tell you what the Lord showed me about you." He turned to face her. He took both her hands in his and looked straight in her eyes. " 'Thou art all fair, my love; there is no spot in thee.' That's the verse God showed me for you. You know that in the Bible it talks about spots and blemishes. This verse tells me there is not a single blemish in you. You are perfect the way God made you."

Anna could hardly believe her ears, but her spirit heard and drank in every word. They were an added balm on her wounded heart, to help finish the healing the Lord had already started.

"Yes."

Once again Anna's voice spoke in a whisper. August wondered what she meant.

"What?"

"Yes." This time when Anna answered, it was stronger. Then she laughed, her voice playing a melody in his heart. "I would like to be courted by you."

August could hardly believe it. She had agreed. This was wonderful! He had thought it would take longer.

"I mean right away." He saw the stars twinkling in Anna's eyes, even though they were under the shade of the tree.

"Right away would be nice." Her shy smile touched his heart.

August didn't want to return to the party, but he knew

they had been outside as long as they should. This time he danced every dance with her. He never took his eyes off her, but she didn't seem to mind. Tomorrow, the courtship would start in earnest.

fifteen

When August arrived home that night, he fell to his knees and dropped his head into his hands. "Help me be what Anna needs, Lord. Show me the best ways to express my love to her. I've waited so long."

The next morning, he didn't go to the smithy first. After breakfast, he drove the wagon back to Gustaf's. On the way, he noticed that the open fields between town and the house were full of wild flowers. He was glad he had walked over to pick up the wagon the day before. On his way back into town, he gathered colorful blossoms. Instead of going to his place of business, he went to the Dress Emporium. It wasn't open, so he climbed the stairs to the apartment. Each step built his anticipation for glimpsing Anna's lovely face again. Had it only been a few hours since he had seen her? It felt like an eternity.

Gerda answered his knock. August peeked around the large bouquet and winked at her. She stepped back.

"Anna, it's for you," she called, turning toward the dining room.

❧

Anna set her cup of tea on the table and went into the parlor. A rather large bouquet filled the doorway and hid whoever was carrying it. Black-eyed Susans, butterfly flowers, wild geraniums, trillium, and columbine—some of her favorites. She put her hand to her chest to still the fluttering of her heart. Without seeing him, she knew it had to be August. He was aware of how much she liked wild flowers. It was one of the things they discussed on one of his many trips to visit her at the shop. The only way he could have gotten those was to pick them this morning. She could picture him walking through a field of wild flowers, filling his arms with the multicolored blossoms. No one had ever before done anything like that for her.

"Come in, August. Would you like a cup of tea, or should I make you some coffee?" Anna's voice sounded breathless, but she couldn't help it. He could think whatever he wanted to about that.

When he stepped over the threshold, Anna thought that she would like to have him in her home every day. . .for the rest of her life. She only hoped their love was strong enough to last that long.

Gerda offered to take the flowers and put them in a vase. "If we have one large enough," she said with a chuckle.

August slid his hands into the front pockets of his jeans. Anna wondered why he was nervous today. She wanted to make him feel comfortable. "You didn't say whether you wanted tea or coffee."

He glanced toward the dining room. "Whatever you and Gerda are having is fine."

Anna nodded. "We're finishing our breakfast with a cup of tea." She led the way to the table. "Have a seat. I think there's another cup in the teapot, if that's what you want."

"Tea'll be fine."

❧

After the wonderful time they had over tea, August came to the Dress Emporium at noon with a picnic basket. While they were visiting that morning, Anna and Gerda had told him how busy they were. He decided that they might like to spread a picnic on the table in the workroom. That way the young women wouldn't have to take time from their work to prepare the noon meal.

When Anna helped August put the tablecloth that he had packed in the basket on the cutting table, their hands brushed. His touch was light as a feather, but it caused excitement to zing up her arm. She quickly glanced at his face. He looked as surprised as she felt. Maybe he had felt a spark, too. She hoped so.

In addition to eating the wonderful food, the three friends laughed and joked a lot.

"I didn't know you could cook, August." Anna grinned up at him. "You might make someone a good wife."

August almost choked on the piece of fried chicken he was chewing. "A good wife?"

She laughed. "Yes, you could do the cooking and clean up the kitchen." She reached for another hot roll.

He had a thoughtful look on his face when he took her hand in his. "I wish I could cook if it would make you happy, Anna, but Mrs. Olson prepared this lunch for me."

Oh, August, you make me happy. Anna wished she were brave enough to say the words, but she wasn't. . .at least, not yet.

Not only did August come at noon, he came to the store after he finished work. He asked if there was any way he could help them. He looked at Anna when he asked the question, but Gerda put him to work carrying crates of new fabrics from the storeroom to the showroom. A new shipment had arrived on the morning train. The stationmaster delivered them right after noon, but Gerda and Anna hadn't had time to unpack the merchandise.

Gerda came back into the workroom. "Anna, why don't you show August where you want the bolts of fabric placed." She sat down and started sewing lace on a blouse.

Anna wondered if Gerda was giving her and August time to be alone. When she stepped into the front room, he had set the final wooden crate on top of the stack.

"Do you have a crowbar to open these?" He leaned one arm on the top box. "I'll do it for you."

She had been opening crates ever since they opened the Dress Emporium, but she was glad he wanted to do it for her. She told him where he would find the tool in the storage room. While he was gone, she walked to the front window and looked out at the busy street. Litchfield was growing, and every day activity increased. An ice cream shop had opened down the block. Of course, all the new people coming into town gave her and Gerda a lot of business, and she was glad.

Soon her mind filled with the man who was helping her. *Lord, I love him so much.* If only her heart was at peace. Her thoughts were interrupted by August returning. Immediately, he started opening the top crate. It was full of bolts of silk.

"Anna, maybe you should unpack this. I'm afraid all the calluses on my hands would snag it. It's too pretty to damage."

She turned around and glanced at him standing beside the counter. Tall and strong with blond hair and those penetrating eyes that changed color to match what he wore. Looking at him caused her heart to beat faster. He was thoughtful in so many ways. His tender side balanced his virility. Why hadn't she seen it sooner? What would her life have been like if he had been the first man to seek her out?

After helping her unpack the crates, he asked her if he could pick her up for church the next Sunday. "Monday, I'm going to Minneapolis to buy a buggy. I don't want to take you anywhere else in a farm wagon. You deserve to ride in style."

❧

When August went to the station to catch the eastbound

train, he was surprised to see Anna and Gerda waiting for him on the platform. It was more pleasant waiting for the train to arrive since they were there, especially Anna. But the wait wasn't long enough. The loud train was right on schedule. It was the first time in his life he wished for his ride to be late.

Before he boarded the car, he took Anna's hands in his. "Thank you for coming. I should be home in a couple of days."

Anna reached up and placed a light kiss on his cheek. Then she blushed and turned around. Gerda stood back and smiled.

On the long ride, August had time to think about that kiss. During the whole time, the spot on his face still felt the imprint of her soft lips. It didn't matter that the touch had been as fleeting as the flutter of a butterfly's wings. Anna had kissed his cheek. He knew it was a silly thought, but he didn't even want to wash his face. He was afraid the feeling would go away. If only they were already married. He wished he was going to return to their home instead of a lonely room in the boardinghouse.

Minneapolis had grown since the last time he was there, and across the river, the state capital of St. Paul was equally bustling. August couldn't keep from thinking of the many new directions his life had taken. As a boy in Sweden, he would never have imagined that as an adult, he would be a blacksmith in the state of Minnesota in the middle of the great country, the United States of America. He would raise his family here, but someday, he wanted to take them back to the land where he had been born. They needed to know their heritage.

While he shopped for the right buggy, August learned a lot about what was going on in the rest of the world. There were major changes in transportation, and he wasn't sure he was ready for all of them.

❧

Anna began to worry when August hadn't returned by Thursday evening. What if there was a train wreck, and he was hurt? But she knew if that was true, the news would have reached Litchfield by now. However, something could have happened to him in Minneapolis. Or driving the buggy home. She whispered a prayer for his safety several times during the day, and she couldn't go to sleep that night. She had tried. She really had, but sleep eluded her.

Finally, Anna got out of bed and pulled on her housecoat. After tying the sash, she stood by her window, watching the quiet street below, soaking up the peacefulness of midnight. The whistle of the westbound train whined in the distance. She almost wished August hadn't left town. She didn't mind riding in a farm wagon with him if that meant he was all right. Her attention was drawn to movement at the end of the street. The shiny paint of a large black surrey glinted in the moonlight. The light was so bright that she could see the red fringe that decorated the roof. A beautiful black stallion pulled the buggy, and August sat on the seat.

Anna smiled to herself. *Thank You, Lord.* Suddenly, Anna yawned, and her eyes felt heavy. She settled into bed with a satisfied sigh. August was home, and all was well.

Because August had so much work waiting for him, it was Friday evening before Anna saw him. He came into the Dress Emporium right before closing time. Anna looked up when the door opened.

"Are you through for the day?" August's voice floated across the room to caress her ears.

"Just about. Why?" Anna couldn't take her eyes off his imposing figure in nice trousers and a white shirt. She wondered why he was dressed like that. She was more used to seeing him in denim trousers or overalls and a plaid work shirt.

"I want to take you for a ride in my new surrey." When August smiled at her, Anna could hardly catch her breath. She had never felt this way before. What was wrong with her?

While they stood there staring at each other, Gerda walked in. "August, when did you get back?" She rushed across the room and hugged him.

Anna wished that she could have done that. She remembered the night of the dance. He had held her in his arms under the tree, while they talked. It felt good. . .and so right.

"What are you doing here all dressed up?" Gerda voiced the question in Anna's mind.

August looked above Gerda's head to where Anna was standing. "I came to take Anna for a ride."

"So go, both of you." Gerda made a shooing motion with her hands. "I can close the store by myself."

❧

Anna started patting her hair the way women did when they thought something was out of place. August thought she looked wonderful, but he would give her time to freshen up if she wanted to.

"I need to go get the horse and buggy. I'm keeping them in Gustaf's barn until the livery stable is rebuilt." He smiled into Anna's eyes that looked green today to match her dress. "I'll be back to pick you up in a few minutes. Is that all right?"

Anna nodded. "Come to the apartment to get me." She followed him out the door.

When August returned, Anna was waiting in the parlor.

They went down to the new vehicle standing by the boardwalk.

"It's beautiful, August." Anna clasped her hands. "So shiny. And the horse matches it so well."

Soon they were heading out of town. The slight breeze increased as the horse picked up speed. Anna gave a tiny shiver, and August pulled her toward him.

"I missed you while I was gone," he whispered against her hair. It was a good thing the horse was well trained, because August didn't want to have to pay that much attention to him.

"I missed you, too." Anna pulled away from him a little. "Actually, I was worried about you. I was afraid something bad had happened, since you took so long to come home."

He laughed. He knew this showed how much she cared. "I didn't want to worry you. It took me longer than I thought it would to find the right surrey and horse."

She smiled and moved back closer to him. "Tell me about Minneapolis."

August told her about all the new things he had seen in the large city. "I even had to go into St. Paul to find the right horse. And do you know what I saw there?"

"No, what?"

"A horseless carriage."

Anna looked puzzled. "What is a horseless carriage?"

"Someone took a buggy and put an engine on it. It ran without having a horse pull it."

Since it was almost dark, August didn't want to go too far from town. At a crossroads, he turned the buggy around and headed back. "I don't think anything will come of it, even though people told me that a lot of those contraptions are being used in France. It was very noisy. It scared the horses. I can't ever imagine it sharing the roadways here with the dependable horses we have."

❧

August often came to take Anna for a ride. The more time they spent together, the more she fell in love with him. His kindness and devotion touched a place in her heart that hadn't ever been touched before. Not by Gustaf, not even by Olaf. Hardly a day went by when August didn't come by for lunch or dinner. Even Gerda had started setting a place for him when she was the one preparing the meal.

Anna began thinking about what marriage to a man like August would mean. The dream of a husband and family that she had decided was not God's plan for her became more possible every day. She could imagine strong sons like their father and a few girls who would be tall like her. The more she thought about these things, the less her heart hurt, until one morning she awoke with the knowledge that all the old pain was totally gone.

❧

About two weeks after August asked Anna if he could court her, he went to the mercantile for supplies.

"I know you like books." Marja glanced over toward the bookshelf display. "We have some new ones."

August decided to browse through them before he returned home. There were several novels he hadn't read, but the book that caught his eye was *Sonnets from the Portuguese* by Elizabeth Barrett Browning. When he opened it, he found that it was not a recent publication, but he hadn't ever seen it before. It was bound in the same leather as the Emily Dickinson book he had bought Anna, but it had an added ribbon bookmark bound into it. When he opened it to the marked page, these words caught his eye. *How do I love thee?*

Let me count the ways.

By the time he finished the poem, he knew that he had to buy this book for Anna. A plan began to form in his mind.

After Marja Braxton wrapped the parcel for him, he took it into the dress shop. Anna was waiting on a customer in the front room. He walked around studying the displays until she was finished.

Then he went to the counter and leaned on it to get closer to Anna. "I have something for you."

She smiled. "I wondered what you were looking for as you walked all over the shop. I thought you were familiar with everything in here. And I was sure you didn't need any of that lace you were studying so intently."

He put the package on the counter between them. "When you open this, please read what's on the page where the bookmark is. I'll be back to pick you up after work. We're going for a ride."

❧

Anna shook her head. The man swaggered as he went out of the store. And he didn't ask if she would go riding with him today. He told her. She waited for the old feelings of being controlled to come over her. But they didn't. She had come to know August's heart. He wasn't overbearing. If he said they were going for a ride, there must be a good reason. She knew he would never intentionally do anything to hurt her. She couldn't help wondering what he was planning.

No one was in the shop, so she went to the workroom. Gerda had gone to the post office, so she was alone. She tore the paper off the book and opened it to the page August told her to read. After the first line, she read slowly to let the words soak into her heart. It expressed how she felt about him, too. The words *freely. . .purely. . .passion. . .smiles. . .tears* touched something deep in her heart that had never been reached before. Once again, she read every word. They were so beautiful, and August wanted her to read them for a reason. Thoughts of what that reason could be brought excitement bubbling up from the depths of her heart. She could hardly wait for the ride later that afternoon.

When Gerda returned, Anna told her that she was taking the rest of the day off. She didn't tell her why, even though Gerda looked surprised. When Anna reached the apartment, she went to her wardrobe and looked at all her dresses. Since she was part owner of a dressmaking business, she had more to choose from than most women. She took several out and laid them on the bed. One by one, she picked them up and held them in front of her as she gazed in the looking glass. Finally, she picked a soft green lawn with tiny white flowers and trimmed with lace.

After taking a long soaking bath, she spritzed on some rose water before she dressed. Working deftly with her fingers, she pushed her hair into a pleasing arrangement decorated with a ribbon the same shade as her dress. She thought she would be ready long before August came, but she had just dropped into her rocking chair in the parlor when a soft knock sounded.

She opened the door and caught her breath. August must have spent most of the afternoon getting ready, too. He was smooth shaven, every hair in place. His clothes looked new, and his shoes so shiny that, if she were close enough, she could probably see her reflection in them.

For a moment they stood and looked at each other, then August said in a voice that was husky with emotion, "My Anna. . .you're so beautiful."

They drove out of town toward Lake Ripley. Anna was aware of how their shoulders touched every time the surrey hit a bump. Too bad the buggy had such good springs. She almost wished it was the farm wagon. She liked the feel of August's warm strength when it touched her.

As they rode along, they talked about many things.

"Anna, when you opened the Dress Emporium, you were so. . .strong and forceful." August kept his gaze on the road ahead. "You said that all you wanted was to be a successful businesswoman. Do you still feel that way?"

Anna sighed. "No, August. I really wanted a home and family all along. I just didn't think it would ever happen. I love the store, and I would want to keep the business. . .at least until I have children."

August started around the lake, but he didn't go all the way. Instead he pulled into a copse of trees that shaded them from the evening sun. Anna was glad. The cool breeze off the water would keep them comfortable on the hot summer day. Birds flitted from tree to tree, calling to each other, and dragonflies flew among the reeds that grew in the shallow water nearby.

After stopping the vehicle, August sat there looking at Anna. She could see the love in his eyes, love such as she read about in the poem he had marked.

"I have a question to ask you." He stopped and cleared his throat.

Anna waited for him to continue, listening to the wind as it softly blew through the trees.

When he started again, the words came out in a torrent. "Anna, I have loved you so long. I can't imagine my life without you. I know this is soon after I asked if I could court you, but I can't wait any longer. . . . Will you marry me?"

The words Anna had been waiting for all her life fell into her heart. She had never heard a man declare his love for her so deeply and sincerely. Warmth flooded her, chasing any remnants of the old feelings that were hiding in the hidden corners of her heart. She tried to answer, but her voice wouldn't work, so she nodded, never taking her eyes from his intense gaze.

August reached to pull her into his arms. The strength of his touch comforted and excited her. He lowered his head until their breath mingled. For a moment he hesitated, as if asking her if he could continue, but she closed the distance between their lips. Tentatively, she touched his. Once, twice. The softness and sweetness were more wonderful than she had ever imagined. A kiss given in love was so much more than the one she had received in anger. She could lose herself in the feelings that overcame her.

❧

When Anna touched her lips to his, August thought he was in heaven. He settled his more firmly on hers and poured all his love into the effort. All the longing. All the passion. Everything around them faded. The only reality was Anna in his arms, returning his kiss with a fervency he had never imagined. He wanted it to last forever, but he knew that would not be a good idea. Reluctantly, he pulled back and rested his forehead against hers. It took several minutes for his breathing to return to normal, and he wasn't the only one.

"Did you read the poem?"

"Yes," she whispered and caressed his cheek with the fingers of one hand. "And it spoke to my soul."

"I'm not good with words, but those could have come straight from my heart to yours."

He pulled her closer against his chest and nestled her head against his neck. "Anna, I have yearned for you so many years. And as my older brother told me, I'm not getting any younger. . . . If it isn't all right with you, I'll understand."

Anna waited for him to continue, then she asked. "August, what are you trying to say to me?"

"I want to get married as soon as possible." The words once again tumbled from him. "Please don't make me wait too long."

Anna sat up and laughed. "You have no idea how happy those words make me. I have wanted a man who felt passion for me."

August's laughter burst forth. "That's what you've got, my Anna. *Ja,* that's for sure!"

epilogue

September 21 was a cold autumn day with crisp air and bright sunshine. Anna felt as if God was smiling on her wedding day. So much had happened in the last two months. Their brothers and many of the neighbors had helped August build their new home. They would live between Gustaf and Olina's house and the edge of town. Both of their families had helped them gather enough furniture so they could move into the house tomorrow. God wasn't just smiling on her wedding day, He was smiling on her whole life.

Olina and Gerda had designed a wedding dress that was more beautiful than the one Anna had planned to wear before. As Gerda helped her dress in her finery, she thanked God for giving her such a wonderful man. Finally, she understood that August was the one God had created for her to love. Life had a funny way of leading a person down the wrong path. That was what had happened in Anna's life. Or maybe she had made choices that had helped her go the wrong way, but she was thankful that God had brought her back to the right man. She knew that their life together, with God as the center, would be rich and full. Only a few hours, and they would be man and wife—and her life would never be the same.

Just before the time for the wedding, her father arrived driving August's new surrey. He had insisted that she and her father use it to get to the church. Since Gerda was going to be her bridesmaid, she also rode in the shiny black vehicle with them. When they arrived at the church, almost everyone was already inside.

Her father helped her down from the buggy and proudly walked her through the door. Anna waited until the pastor's wife began playing the pump organ. Then she and her father walked down the aisle toward the man who was the other half of her heart. Love was a beacon shining from his eyes when he looked at her. She was glad that she had chosen to wear a veil. She didn't want August to see the tears in her eyes. He might not understand that they were tears of happiness and joy.

❧

When the organ started playing, August looked at the door at the back of the sanctuary. Anna was covered with a cloud of creamy fabric that was decorated with lace. As she and her father came down the aisle toward him, they looked as if they were floating.

Gud, thank You for giving this woman to me. How could he have ever thought of her as his brother's castoff? She was the best gift God had given him, besides Jesus. She fulfilled all the longings in his heart for a wife and family. He was thankful God had helped him win the battle over jealousy. Now he was free to love Anna the way God wanted her to be loved.

A Letter To Our Readers

Dear Reader:

In order that we might better contribute to your reading enjoyment, we would appreciate your taking a few minutes to respond to the following questions. We welcome your comments and read each form and letter we receive. When completed, please return to the following:

Fiction Editor
Heartsong Presents
PO Box 719
Uhrichsville, Ohio 44683

1. Did you enjoy reading *His Brother's Castoff* by Lena Nelson Dooley?
   ❑ Very much! I would like to see more books by this author!
   ❑ Moderately. I would have enjoyed it more if
   ____
   ____
   ____

2. Are you a member of **Heartsong Presents**? ❑ Yes ❑ No
   If no, where did you purchase this book? ________________
   ____

3. How would you rate, on a scale from 1 (poor) to 5 (superior), the cover design? ________________

4. On a scale from 1 (poor) to 10 (superior), please rate the following elements.

____ Heroine	____ Plot
____ Hero	____ Inspirational theme
____ Setting	____ Secondary characters

5. These characters were special because?________________

____

____

6. How has this book inspired your life?________________

____

____

7. What settings would you like to see covered in future **Heartsong Presents** books? ________________

____

____

8. What are some inspirational themes you would like to see treated in future books? ________________

____

____

9. Would you be interested in reading other **Heartsong Presents** titles? ❑ Yes ❑ No

10. Please check your age range:

❑ Under 18 ❑ 18-24
❑ 25-34 ❑ 35-45
❑ 46-55 ❑ Over 55

Name____
Occupation ___________________________________
Address _____________________________________
City________________ State_______ Zip__________